A Dramatist

Playwriting

A handbook for would-be dramatic authors

A Dramatist

Playwriting
A handbook for would-be dramatic authors

ISBN/EAN: 9783337281700

Printed in Europe, USA, Canada, Australia, Japan

Cover: Foto ©Andreas Hilbeck / pixelio.de

More available books at **www.hansebooks.com**

PLAYWRITING.

PLAYWRITING:

A HANDBOOK

FOR [WOULD-BE

DRAMATIC AUTHORS.

BY

A DRAMATIST.

London :

THE STAGE OFFICE,

Clement's Inn Passage, Strand, W.C.

1888

MACRAE, CURTICE, AND CO., LIM.

PRINTERS,

CLEMENT'S HOUSE, CLEMENT'S INN PASSAGE, LONDON W.C.

CONTENTS.

APPENDIX.

PLANS OF STAGE AND EXPLANATION OF STAGE DIRECTIONS.

PREFACE.

IT was many, **many** years **ago** that *I* began my melancholy career **as a** Dramatic Author; **and a hard** and bitter-fought beginning *I* can **well** remember that **it was**. *I* **was** inexperienced, shy, **and foolish; without money, without influence.** *I* knew **not a single soul connected** even in **the most** distant **way** with the **theatrical world.** *I* **knew no one to advise me or give me a hint.** For years *I* **danced in impotent frenzy around the high strong walls that** guard the city **of Dramatic Art.** *I* **ran** my head against the **stones,** *I* **tore** myself **against the** spiky **gates,** *I* **soused** myself in the **dirty moat,** *I* **screamed and** cursed, **and blubbed.** At last, *I* climbed **over and got in.** *I* don't think **much** of the show now *I* am in; **but that has** nothing to do with **us** here, our object in this little book being merely **to** discuss the question of getting in; and *I* enumerate **the** difficulties that beset me only to show to the struggling young besiegers of to-day **how, with the aid of** pig-headed obstinacy, sublime conceit, **thick** skin, **and a genius for** nagging and boring and worrying **human** people's lives out **of them,** it is possible to force even **so strongly** guarded **a** portal **as the** stage door of the present century.

I also hope to show you how to force that door with less **waste** *of* **time** *and energy than I spent upon the task myself. Many years of* **fretful** *groping, of* **useless** *labour,* **of** *misdirected effort could be saved to most beginners* **by a** *brief* **glimpse** *into that strange* **world** *they hope to win, by a moment's knowledge of its funny little ways, by a passing insight into the character of its curious inhabitants.*

It is this glimpse, this knowledge, this insight, that I propose to give my readers.

Nor *do I anticipate that by so doing I shall be the means of overcrowding* **the Dramatic Market.** *The road that* **leads to** *that* **market is** *a very long* **road, a very** *stoney road, a very uphill road, a* **very** *wearisome* **to the flesh** *and heart-breaking* **to the** *spirit road; and only a few of the many who start—only the very* **strong and** *the* **very** *determined,* **can ever hope** *to reach the other end. Such strength* **and** *determination* **no book can give you.** *All I can hope to do is to guide you along the right path, to save you from* **walking** *at the rate of five miles an hour down the* **wrong lanes, and** *puffing* **and blowing round the wrong turnings.**

THE *AUTHOR.*

PLAYWRITING.

CHAPTER I.

INTRODUCTORY.

I wish it were not so hackneyed a custom, that of quoting *Punch's* advice to people about to marry, and applying it to the particular question in hand, because I wanted to do the very same thing here. I wanted to begin these papers with: "Advice to people about to write plays. Don't." But the idea has been done to death, and so, of course, I can't make use of it.

And it would have been good advice too. Goethe, who, one might think, would have escaped the flints and briars of the literary path if anybody could have done so, said (I am not using the exact words; it is easier to paraphrase than to hunt up a reference), that, if young men only knew what a trying, troublous life an author had to lead, the courts of the Muses would be but sparsely crowded with aspirants. This was spoken of authorship in general, and is certainly true enough of it. But dramatic authorship is to the profession of literature as reversing is to waltzing—an agony within a misery. A man who means to be a dramatist must be prepared for a life of never-ending strife and fret—a brain and heart-exhausting struggle from the hour when, full of hope, he starts off with his first farce in his pocket to the days when, involuntarily taking the advice of one of the early masters of his own craft, to wit, old rare Ben Jonson, he leaves " the loathed stage, and the more loathsome age."

The mere **writing** of a play is generally allowed to be moderately harassing business of itself, but this, if not the last, is at all events the very least of a dramatic author's difficulties. It is only a necessary preliminary, like the catching of the hare before you **jug it.** His real work begins when his three or four acts are neatly "typed " out, and tied up with red tape. When, after months, **perhaps** years, of hawking it about from pillar to post—and **very wooden**-headed posts some of them are—of trotting attendance here, of waiting attendance there, of urging and **scheming elsewhere, it is, at length,** accepted, even then he is not **much nearer the goal of production** than he was before ; for, if **the proverb " There's many a slip 'twixt** cup and lip " should **be kept in mind more constantly by any** one class than another in this uncertain sphere, it is by those having business in connection **with the British drama. The** glorious uncertainty **of the turf, the fascinating fickleness of** woman, the interesting **variableness of the weather, fade into insignificance** beside the **magnificent unreliableness of all** theatrical arrangements and **affairs. But that I do not** care to tell the secrets of my prison-house, I **could tales unfold—tales** of disappointments and **delays, of hopes deferred, of chances** dashed from the grasp at the **very moment they seemed** clutched, of weary waitings **rewarded by failure, of enterprise and** effort leading only to **defeat, of hard work winning** only loss—tales whose lightest **word would harrow up the soul** of the would-be dramatist, **freeze his young blood, and** make his each particular hair to **stand on end. But this theatrical blazon must** not be to

ears outside the Profession. Nor need **it be.** **There is no**
necessity to go behind the scenes to gather proof **of** the **doubt**
and indecision **that** spread like a baneful fungus over **every**
dramatic flower-bed. Each week the theatrical columns of the
newspapers teem with evidences of the unfortunate fact, and he
who **runs** can read. Let **me cull** a few **examples** from the
records of a past season.* **An announcement** appears **in** the
papers that Mr. Jos. Hatton **and Mr. Wm.** Terriss are writing
a drama for the Adelphi. Messrs. Gatti immediately **reply that**
they know nothing whatever about this. Mr. **Hatton thereupon**
writes that he and Mr. Terriss drafted out **the complete plot of**
a play and read **it to** the Adelphi management, and **that he**
certainly was under the impression **that** it had been **virtually**
accepted, and that nothing remained but to fill in the dialogue.
This is the last heard of the business. Reflection :—What
were and are Mr. Hatton's inward feelings upon the subject ;
ditto Mr. Terriss'. Again, and in connection with **the** same
house, it was understood that Mr. Geo. R. Sims—not a young
beginner to whom disappointment would come **like** mother's
milk—was collaborating **with Mr. Pettitt in a piece to follow**
The Harbour Lights. Then **came** news that **that** arrangement
was off, and that the next production would be **from** the pen of
Messrs. Grundy and Pettitt. Then, that Messrs. Grundy and
Pettitt's piece—written, accepted, and settled for—has been
indefinitely postponed, and that a revival of *Peep o' Day* was to
be put on during the autumn, and **that** Messrs. Grundy **and**
Pettitt were not altogether pleased about the business—a **sur-**
mise well within the pale of belief. As for the making and
upsetting of plans at the Globe during the same season referred
to, the mind grows dizzy at contemplation of them. A new
comedy, by Geo. P. Hawtrey, entitled *I.O.U.* is to follow *The*

---

* 1886-7. 1786-7 would have done just as well as a sample. 1986-7 **will**
produce a precisely similar state of affairs.

Pickpocket. Out comes *The Lodgers.* *I.O.U.* is to follow *The Lodgers.* A new farcical comedy by Mr. Grundy is to follow *The Lodgers.* Mr. F. C. Burnand is adapting *La Doctoresse* for the Globe, and the piece will be put on in a week or two. Out comes a revival of *The Snowball.* Mr. Grundy's new piece will follow *The Snowball.* Mr. Burnand's adaptation of *The Doctoresse* will follow *The Snowball.* Mr. Hawtrey is in treaty for a new farce by Manville Fenn and J. H. Darnley. Then more talk of Grundy's piece, and then, after all this groaning, the mountain produces a revival of *The Private Secretary.* To follow *The Secretary,* a new farcical comedy by W. Lestocq and Walter Everard was in active production. Instead of that, we had at last *The Doctor.* Put yourself, my dear reader, in the place of Mr. Geo. P. Hawtrey, of Mr. Grundy, of Mr. Manville Fenn, of Mr. Lestocq, of Mr. Walter Everard, and imagine that your brilliant comedy, after dangers and difficulties innumerable, all happily surmounted, had at last been accepted, and was, as you fondly imagined, on the eve of production, that you had told all your friends about it, and they had congratulated you, and had hoped, with somewhat unnecessary anxiety, that it would be a success, and you had, in anticipation of your forthcoming wealth, ordered a new hat, and had airily hinted to your tailor that he could send his bill in if he liked (if *he* liked !), and that, indeed, matters were so far forward and so firmly fixed that you had sent round announcements to the papers, a thing you would not do until you felt your footing pretty certain for fear of being laughed at afterwards. And the next morning, Hey Presto ! all your substantial looking castle has tumbled down about your ears, and you are standing, half blinded, in the dust and dirt of its ruins.

Call to mind the announcements and counter-announcements regarding nearly every theatre in London, and the same ghastly spectre of uncertainty is conjured up before you. At the Princess's a new romantic drama by Henry Herman was to have been brought out in the spring. What has become of that?

These are all recent instances, examples drawn from **the** 1886-7 season. But the tale has ever been the same. I have before me old programmes, announcing dozens upon dozens of forthcoming productions **in** the most **particular** and positive manner, not one of which has ever seen the light. To speak of more recent times, what has become of the *Hypatia* that a well-known London journalist had written for Mary Anderson? When is Mr. Irving going to produce that piece which **Mr.** Frank Marshall told us some years ago was in his **hands?** Where **is** *Theodora,* **twice** on the eve of being played **at the** Princess's? Take in *The Stage,* my dear young reader, **and cut** out the announcements each week of plays that are being written, of plays that have been accepted, of plays that are about to be produced. Paste them all into a book, **and** when one is played —no matter whether it be a success or a failure, that is another matter altogether—put a tick against it. When a year, say, has gone by, and nothing has been heard of another, put a cross against that other, and compare, as you go **on, the** number of ticks with the number of crosses. And remember that each cross represents a very heavy heart being carried about for many **a** long day under somebody or other's waistcoat—tells that somebody or other feels very sick and cold down the back as he moves about his little world, trying to appear careless and to laugh it off—that somebody or other feels very tired and weary of the struggle, and almost wishes now and then that it were over.

And **if** such are the discomfitures and defeats of men who have already fought their way into the dramatic citadel—of men like those I have referred to, who are **all** known, and more or **less** influential in theatrical circles—if such are their disappointments what, think you, must be the struggles and heartbreakings of the young beginners—of the nameless fighters, who with no friend within to show them **a** ladder, with no golden key to unlock the iron gates, are **tearing** their **hands** against the jagged walls without ?

Their disappointment cannot be traced by reference **to** **programmes and** paragraphs in Theatrical Chit Chat. *Their* failures **upon failures,** *their* daily repulses, *their* broken hopes are **known only to the one** pet **sister, the** one staunch chum. But **you may be** sure that for every single buffet **among the one group** there are fifty knock-down **blows among** the other.

Therefore it is that I feel it my duty to advise you not to try to 'become a dramatist.

Not that I expect for a moment that you will follow my advice. Not that I should respect you much if you did. Every profession has its drawbacks. Every state of life into which you are called, or into which you push your way, without waiting to be called, has its anxieties and perplexities. But to every workman his own **trade appears the most undesirable of all ; and if you wait to enter a calling until those already in it recommend it to you, you will sit and twiddle your thumbs till grave-time. A baker sees all the disadvantages incident to a** bakehouse, **and imagines a butcher's business is all smooth sailing.** Play-writing **seems to me a thing to be shunned and escaped from ; but,** were I a lawyer, **there is little** doubt but **that, like all the solicitors I know, I should warn young men against** entering **the law ; and had I adopted the profession of a** chimneysweep, **I expect I should never weary of telling people to** be anything but **that, and** of expatiating on **the discomforts of early** rising, and **the sinful- ness of** smoke-consuming **grates.**

I knew a young man once who thought he would go on the stage, and he mentioned the idea to some friends of his who were in the business, and they talked to him, and told him things about an actor's life, till he couldn't go to sleep of nights for terror, so he gave up the notion of being an actor, and determined to become a doctor, which was, perhaps, not so pleasant, but more practicable. And he consulted the family physician on the subject, and a cousin, **who was** an army surgeon, and **he** also explained **his** intention **to** a couple of old schoolfellows in London ; and they just opened his **eyes** to the thing a bit, and he saw clearly that the professions were all done for, and must soon come to an end. **So he** made up his mind not to bother about ambition, but to keep a small shop **and live** comfortably. And he asked the local tradesmen what **would be** the **best** sort of shop for him **to keep,** and they recommended him not **to keep** any shop at all, **but to buy** two yards of good stout rope **and hang** himself, because **that** was what he'd have to do in the end, if he did keep a shop ; **and** that, if he did it at the beginning, he'd save the shop's keep during the intervening period. Then he concluded that he might just **as** well be an actor after all. He **is** doing remarkably well now.

Be a dramatist, **my** young **friend, if you feel** you have any talent in that direction, and possess the pluck **to** fight down the hundred difficulties that will **confront** you at every step, the endurance to stand firm against **the** hundred disappointments that will surge round you at **every point.** You will, **if** you are careful to look fairly at your own **work** with clear mental **eye**-sight, and not gloat over it through the microscope of **conceit,** soon discover whether you have any real dramatic ability **or not.** If not, by all means quit the business promptly, for the most you will accomplish, in such case, will be to gain the position of a theatre hack—grinding out childish drivel, and earning thereby, at tremendous cost of labour, an average but uncertain **income** of from a hundred to **two** hundred a year.

If, however, you have dramatic talent, it would be wicked, **in** the present state of affairs, not to let the British stage have the benefit **of it** ; and if you can put together anything better than a hotch-potch of old scenes and incidents, explained in language that no human being was ever known to employ off the stage, and enlivened by wit of that character which is usually **asso**-ciated with a horse collar, the public—which **has been a** long while waiting for you—will, you may be sure, **welcome and reward** you right royally.

Therefore, I say again, that if you want **to be a dramatist by all** means try; and if you will follow me to the next chapter, we will **discuss the making of** the play which **you are to** thunder at **the** dingy portal **of the Thespian Castle wherein the** Princess **Fame lies** captive.

But mind! if things *do* **turn out** wrong; **if time and** labour **are both** wasted; if only failures crown your efforts, and you **come** back from the field wounded **and** o'erthrown, remember, please, **that** I knew very **well how 'twould be,** and that *I told you so*!

This reflection will, I feel, be a consolation to you.

CHAPTER II.

MANY, many years ago, there appeared in **the** columns of a certain theatrical journal, published in a far-off land, a series of papers written by a certain youthful but eminent dramatic author of that period and country, upon the art of writing plays. I did not travel to that far-off land to read those articles because, being a dramatic author myself, I naturally doubted the possibility of any other dramatic author knowing anything worth listening to upon the subject. But people not so clever as I am —mere ordinary mortals—who did read those articles in those ancient days, told me that they were excellent, and that they explained the whole matter so explicitly and thoroughly that any person of common intelligence, who had studied them, ought to be able to sit down then and there and write a brilliant comedy ; and indeed, so unreservedly did that youthful but eminent dramatist give himself away, and so recklessly did he lay bare the secrets of his art, that older and more selfish playwrights began to grow alarmed.

" My boy," said they, kindly but reproachfully, " My boy, isn't it rather foolish of you to go telling everyone how to write plays ? We shall have the market glutted with stirring dramas and side-splitting comedies if you go on in this way. And prices will go down, and we shall all be edged off our perches. Don't do it."

And that youthful but eminent personage began to see himself that he had been rather foolish. But, as he said, the mischief was done then.

And yet I have not noticed that since that time the public has been any the more, what one may call, surfeited with great plays than it was before, or that the quality of plays in general has to any noticeable extent been improved.

This may seem strange on first consideration, but, perhaps, it is that the dramatic art, like poetry and spelling, is one of those things that cannot be learned, but which must be born in a party. A man that needs to be told how to write a play, it is useless telling, for he will never write one, and a man that can write a play does not need to be told how to do it. It is a case of instinct not experience. One hears a good deal of nonsense talked (ye gods and little fishes—whatever that exclamation may imply—what a deal of nonsense one does hear talked in this world !) of the necessity of "training" for a dramatic author, and solemn idiots write pompous articles about the presumption of any person under the age of seventy-five attempting to write for the stage. They insist upon the necessity of young men spending the freshest and strongest part of their lives patiently waiting to grow old, and, meanwhile, studying the great modern English dramatists; as if insight into human nature and dramatic inspiration were, like blindness and dotage, merely a question of years. Dion Boucicault wrote *London Assurance* before he was eighteen, and in nine cases out of ten an author's first work is the best he ever turns out. The fancy soars far higher in youth than in age, and tears flow freer and laughter rings brighter at twenty-five than at fifty.

Nor do you need a knowledge of Greek tragedy and an intimate acquaintance with the dramatic literature of the Restoration, to write a play that will move **the** hearts that are beating beside yours to-day. A book-worm never made a great author. The mouldering thought of a buried age, the tale told for **a** generation that has passed away, will be but little use to you, if you wish to do work for **the** boards, and not for the shelves. The living life around you is your book, **and** your **brain is your** teacher. Learn from them.

A nature capable of **vibrating to the** whole gamut of human passion and emotion ; **a** sympathy so wide and deep that there is room for all humanity upon its bosom, from the little lovesick maiden **to the** stern strong man, from the castle dreaming boy to the fretful beldam, from the yokel to the statesman, from the strumpet to the saint ; **a** mental vision that will pierce the murderer's heart, **the** hero's soul, and lay **bare** their inmost thoughts before you ; a never-failing instinct that will reveal to you the one dramatic moment in each **scene of life ; the** artist's inborn art that alone can teach you how to show to others what you see—these qualifications and these qualifications only will you need to become a dramatic author.

I do not, however, teach them.

But although it is not possible to learn how to write poetry, even a Milton must master the rules of verse ; and, though dramatists cannot be turned out like barristers and carpenters, still a Shakespeare must go through a school. You must acquire the technical skill as well as possess the natural talent for the work.

Unfortunately for you, however, the laws of the drama, though as strong and as impossible to sail against as is the shifting wind, are as impalpable and as invisible as is the air. You will not find them stored in any handbook, you will not hear them from the lips of any master. I could roll off fifty or a hundred neatly-turned instructions for you here, but they would no more teach you to write a play than a treatise on navigation would help a landsman to handle a yacht. Beyond a few rudimentary hints and technical rules, which we will discuss hereafter, nothing can be taught, no help can be given.

Then what the blazes, you naturally ask in your common, **vulgar** way, **am I** writing this chapter for? My boy, I will **tell you.** Carlyle said truly that the greatest thought was the thought **that made men think. I am going to teach** you the greatest of teaching, **according to that same principle :** I am going to teach you how to learn.

Attend the theatres **constantly. See all plays (Heaven help you !).** Read what is written and listen to what is said of them afterwards. Note which are **successful,** and think **out** why they **are successful. Note those that fail, and** worry it out until you see **clearly why it was that they did fail. Watch** the play as a young bird watches the **early flight of its** mother. Analyse it scene by scene as a chemical **student** analyses **a new drug. Note in** each what it is that most holds you. Remember, when **you are** musing over **it** afterwards, what **it was that bored you. If** a situation grips your **entire senses, keeps you** breathless with **excitement and suspense,** and leaves you at the end thoroughly delighted **or deeply thoughtful, do not** forget that situation in a hurry—not, **at all events, until** you have dissected every line of it, until its whole anatomy **lies bare before you, and you can** trace its structure **up from the point where your attention was** first arrested **to the precipice whereon it culminated.**

If, on the other **hand, the situation** seemed as **though it** ought to have aroused **you, and yet did not, examine into it** until you grasp the **reason why it missed its mark.** If the situation itself was **powerful, then it must** have been the clumsy building **up** that **marred it, in which case** study that clumsy building up **so as to avoid it. If the scene,** however, was well **constructed, and yet fell flat—which will be rare,** for, in literature, **it is the workmanship far more than the material** that tells ; a skilful writer obtaining a stronger effect **out of a** broken promise than an unskilful one will out of **a couple of** murders and a forgery—then the motive must have been **weak indeed, and you** will remember what that motive was.

Note, in good plays, how the scenes follow one another, how quiet and playful ones generally **precede** passionate **ones—a** thunderstorm following immediately upon a hurricane would not be impressive—and how tempest is succeeded by calm. Note how delay, as in the scene after the murder of Duncan, in Macbeth, carried to a certain point, spurs anticipation ; how, carried beyond that point, **it** only aggravates. Note all entrances and exits, how they are managed ; the excuses that take people off the stage when they **are** not wanted ; the circumstances causing seventeen total strangers to one another, each residing in an entirely different part of the globe, to be for ever turning up together in the same spot, and mark what appears sensible **and** what appears so absurd **as to** spoil your interest in the whole **scene.**

Note, above all things, **how the story is** told and the suspense maintained. Observe—when you **get** the chance—how the interest, set rolling early in the first act, and gathering force at every scene, leaps forward, without pause, from act to act, till the grand catastrophe **is** reached ; and solve the method by which this is done very carefully indeed, for such a play will be an ideal play, and, if you can construct another like it, there will be a big fortune in it for you.

Study, particularly, every example you can find, bearing on that vexed question as to whether the audience should be taken into your confidence or be surprised. Is is a question that can never be decided, and you must choose for yourself. For my own part, I am inclined to favour the confidence trick. The interest of an audience is not in their curiosity but in their expectation. In *Hamlet* they know the whole story by the end of the first act. After that they are merely waiting for what they feel must happen—the death **of** Claudius **at** the hand of his murdered brother's son.

Beginners, at all events, I should strongly advise against working on the surprise method. It is certainly false art, and though some startling effects may now and then have been obtained from it, these have been won always by old, experienced hands. As a rule, the attempt has resulted in failure.

Go and see a really good play over and over again (no, I do not get any commission), studying it from a different point of view each time. Give your whole attention one night to the story and how it is treated as a whole; another time, examine the construction, that is, the arrangement of the scenes and acts; a third time, note the situations and the way they are worked up; a fourth, the dialogue; a fifth, the characters; a sixth, the minor details of movement and positions, and so on; and upon everything you see and note, endeavour to improve.

Do not read plays. Having the print of a piece before you while recalling to mind its representation is very useful in assisting your analysis, but do not be content with reading merely. There is a vast difference between a play acted and a play read, the inability to perceive, which stands much in the way of would-be dramatists, and your business is with the former, not with the latter. Familiarise yourself with how things look on the stage, not how they read by the fireside. Get so acquainted with the stage that you will be able to conjure up a vision of it at will ; that, while writing, you will see, through your half-closed eyes, the curtained opening with the lighted scene beyond, and your puppets fretting out their dream life thereupon ; see them pacing gracefully its air-built floor ; see them fiercely fronting and defying one another; kneeling gently to their mistresses, standing crushed with mute despair, flying at their false foe's throat, sobbing out their sorrows on their lovers' breast, dying with a curse upon their lips—" left centre, down stage.''

CHAPTER III.

PLAYWRITING *(continued)*.

THEATRE GOING, too, besides making you acquainted with the drama's laws, will—more important still—make you acquainted with and enable you to understand the likes and dislikes of those who make the drama's laws, to wit, the drama's patrons. Go to the pit (I take it, of course, **that you are not a** snob, with objections to "anything common"). **The** gallery is useful for **a** change, but is, as a rule, **too noisy and** inattentive. The dress circle is "young personny" and respectable. **It** giggles **at all the** love scenes, and murmurs, "Oh, isn't he nice!" whenever the hero appears. The stalls chatter, and regard the play as **a nuisance. It is from the** pit that you get **the idea of the** general public taste.

And do not despise public taste in that haughty, youthful **way of** yours, because that's silly. It is the fashion among bad workmen of all trades, who imagine that their want of success must be due to anything and everything rather than to themselves, to sneer at their employers; but, as a matter of fact, the public are far better judges of art than the "artistic" cranks **who** abuse them. The Lyceum, ever since Irving took the **management** of it, **has been** the most steadily patronised theatre in London. *Lohengrin*, which your superior " artistic" folk would have strangled at its birth, has grown to be one of the most popular of all operas. *Lady Clancarty* and *Dandy Dick* were both immense draws ; while—well, some of the theatres do not do very well sometimes, and their not doing so is another pretty clear proof of the correctness of public taste.

Therefore do not grumble at public taste, but rather follow it. I do not mean pander to it. It must be left to your own good judgment to distinguish between its healthy appetite and its sick fancies. .

A first night pit, the first three rows of it, will be your best guide. The critics merely echo more or less the voice of the house, and the six feet behind the stalls is the mouth through which that voice is heard. Sit there, and understand the thought around you. Mark what goes down with them, and what they grow restless at and cough through. It is wonderful what an index to an audience's mind their cough is. They can sit in direct draughts with their clothes wet through all the evening, and take no harm, but a prosy scene brings on an epidemic of bronchitis sufficient to lay half of them in their graves. You will find—what, if you have any dramatic talent, you will not need to learn—that it is action, not talk, that arouses and holds an audience. Drama means action. A grip of the hand, a look, a sob, tells an audience more than twelve pages of dialogue could explain. Silence is the eloquence of drama. Avoid long speeches, especially those that have nothing to do with the play. A theatrical audience does not care two-pence for poetical descriptions of moonlight, and treatises on social problems. If you want to display your "fine writing" put it into essays or poems. Anyhow, keep it out of your stage-work. *Harvest* would have been a success, I am confident, if it had not been for the magnificent lectures on Bohemia, old age, Scotch law, and every other chance topic that happened to arise.

Plays **of this kind** always remind me of those frauds **they** used to **palm** off upon me in my boyish **days as stories, where** Tommy would go for a walk with his **mother and ask questions** on scientific subjects—the blithering young **idiot!—and be** answered in two pages of **useful** information.

You will find they want their drama strong. **Idyllic themes** must, if employed at all, be confined to one-act pieces. **Modern** theatre-goers will not accept **two** hours of **them.** *Young Mrs. Winthrop* is a **lovely piece,** but weak in motive, and **it did not** draw.

Audiences are not—to their credit—partial **to** maudliness. Eschew broken-hearted maidens and love-sick youths as heroes and heroines. They love not cynicism except as flavouring **to** "heart."

They are not too much troubled about probability, provided possibility is not outraged. But the more reasonable things are why of course the better. They will "make believe" with you that a man would never recognise his wife in somebody else's hat, and they take in law that would make Blackstone, if he heard it, turn in his grave. But they would be glad of a change in these respects. *Verb sap.*

Audiences do not thirst, as young beginners fancy they do, for exhaustive particulars on points of detail. They accept your premises without any wish to argue the matter. If you tell them that your villain murdered his aunt three years before the play began, they take your word for it, and pass it. This, however, is not sufficient for your young playwright. He must explain why the man killed his aunt, how he killed his aunt, and what the uncle said about it. In *Barbara* it was necessary to the play that someone should **have** left Miss B. a fortune. The how, why, when, and by whom it was left were immaterial. But Mr. Jerome, in his youthful conscientiousness, evidently felt he had not done his duty by us until he had given us the history of Barbara's aunt, and the early life and adventures of

c

Barbara's mamma.   **It was the one** weak **point of** the play.

And now for the few practical instructions before hinted **at.**

Do not put important matter into the first few lines of an act. There is always a bustle and buzz as **the** curtain goes up and the house settles down, and the opening speeches are half lost. **Let** them be like the opening bars of **an** overture—**a mere** call **to** attention.   **Do not, if you can avoid** it, have your leading people **" discovered."   The actors do not** like it.   They **do not** get much applause for being **discovered.**   What they like is for their entrance to **be "led up to."   And,** for the same reason, do **not** bring on **two characters together.**   Each actor thinks the **applause is meant only for him, and it** makes unpleasantness during the whole run of the piece.

While on this branch of the art, remember, too, that actors **prefer entrances and** exits by the centre rather than side ones, **as showing them** off to more advantage.

Every character must have a speech **or an action to** "take **them off,"** and should not **enter a moment** before they are wanted.   **Pay great attention to your** curtain.   In melodrama it should certainly be upon a situation of some sort—the comic man denouncing the villain being the most popular.   In comedy **this** is not **necessary, but, even** there, it should be at some moment of dramatic significance.   In any event, bear **in** mind that it is your **last word, and that** your audience will remember you by it to the exclusion **of everything else that has gone before.**   To them it is **the concentrated summing-up of the whole act.**

To understand the **carpentry** of play-writing, you must be **personally acquainted with the stage.   The grouping,** position, **and movement** of your characters—the correct poising of the picture—is an essential **part of** your work, and, to perform it **properly, you must be at** home among " flats " and " wings," "back-cloths" and "front cloths," half-sets and full sets, "L.2.E." and "R.1.E."* You must be familiar with the technical language of the stage, or you will not be able to explain yourself, and a manager, glancing over your MS., will naturally conclude that you do not know your subject, and will throw the thing aside.

To attempt to become a play-writer without practical experience of the land behind the scenes is like trying to build an easy chair upon a knowledge of cabinet making derived from "Cassell's Popular Recreator." I could explain to you that, as a general rule, the chief action of each scene should take place in the centre, well down stage—that is, near the footlights; that there are certain points at which the actor should take the stage, and others at which he should retire up. I could tell you that a set scene in the middle of an act must be preceded by a front one, and that that front one must not be of a delicate character, as, if so, the noise of the carpenters, building up behind it, would drown it. But it would be like *telling* a man how to swim.

No, you must go upon the stage. If you can afford the time and money, join a country company for a few months, or enter as utility at some small London theatre. An agent will arrange this for you very readily. You must be prepared to keep yourself during this temporary enlistment, and the business, altogether, will cost you, probably, about a hundred pounds. But it will be money well spent. If you cannot manage this plan, go in as a super somewhere. Where there's a will there's a way.

To come back to our playwriting, let me urge you to be, above all things, practicable. A theatre is not a temple of art, but a house of business, and the question that a manager will ask himself when considering whether to accept your piece or not, will be, not how much merit, but how much money there is in it. Keep your grand ideas and your experiments until you

---

* See plans in Appendix.

have got the ear of the public. People must be willing to follow you before you can lead them.

Your early pieces, also, must not be too expensive to produce. A manager cannot be expected to hazard much upon the work of an untried man. Do not begin by writing plays requiring elaborate scenery and heavy casts. Do not ask for the Colosseum by moonlight with view of Rome in the distance. You will only get a "courtyard" with a "mediæval street" backing, if they do take the piece. Simple modern interiors or stock exteriors such as "a country lane," "a street," "fairy glen Llangolfechmaenmawr," should be your aim, and if only one scene to each act so much the better, both from the artistic and the economic point of view. Likewise, do not go in for balls, and swell picnics, and marriages, you will not be able to afford to give large parties until you have made your way.

It is for these thrifty reasons that "curtain raisers" are the very best things for young dramatists to start upon. Costing, comparatively speaking, nothing to put on, and their success or failure not involving any very serious consideration, they form a pretty safe medium by which a manager can test an untried man. They also afford excellent practice, enabling you to feel your way before attempting more ambitious work, and— very important indeed—commencing your career with them gives you a reputation for modesty, and modesty is always a good card to play. That is all I have to say on the subject of play-writing except this, do not, my young would-be dramatist, write five-act blank verse tragedies. I can hardly believe that you do ever write such things, but managers and the comic journals are always saying that you do, and, as they wouldn't tell a lie, I take it that you really do, and, therefore, beg you not to. Do not write either tragedy or blank verse. Both are drugs in the market. Tragedy was all very well in the old earnest ages, but in these frothy, fevered days of *persifiage* men have neither the time, inclination, nor ability to think.

And to put your dialogue into the form of blank verse **is to** hamper yourself for no reason whatever. Blank **verse is only** justifiable for thought so deep and strong that **it falls of** itself into that form. If your thought **is of** that kind **and** fashion **it** is not you whom **I** would presume to teach, and these articles you will pass by from beginning to end with **a smile.** It is only to my younger **brother** workers in the fields of common-place, but, let us hope, honest and well meaning art that I am speaking, and to them I say emphatically **do** not venture on verse. *Our* thought, *our* fancy, ***our*** philosophy **will be** mounted well enough on **prose.** We should only look puny and ridiculous behind the great sweeping wings of Pegasus.

And, indeed, **I** doubt **if the** age would listen to us were we to write the verse of Milton or of Dante ; at all events, not the theatrical age. Shakespeare himself would be cold-shouldered **if** he came trotting round trying to introduce his wares to us **now.** He is appreciated, as **it is,** true ; but how much **of** that appreciation is of understanding, **and** how **much of custom** and fashion ?

Shakespeare **is** an old-established firm, and the public have grown **to** accept him as part of the order of things. They have been brought up to admire and revere him as a religion, and they murmur his praises in the same way that they mumble through the Litany at church, without in the slightest knowing why they do it, or what it is it all means. Had Shakespeare been born thirty and not three hundred years ago his name, instead of being a household word, would be unknown to the public altogether, and familiar—dimly as that of a pestering nuisance—only to the theatrical lessees.

I can well imagine how a London manager would greet our young friend Shakespeare, coming to him in this year of grace one thousand eight hundred and eighty-eight, with the MS. of *Hamlet* under his arm. Let us for a moment conjure up the scene. Let **us** take an imaginary manager, say, the husband of

Mrs. Gamp's ghostly patroness—Mrs. Harris—and listen to the brief interview.

HARRIS (*opening and reading letters, and speaking without turning round*). Well, my boy, what is it? You must be quick; I've only a minute to spare.

SHAKESPEARE (*with a rather meaningless chuckle, nervously twisting his hat the while*). Er-er, 'bout that play of mine, you know. Left it with you 'bout a week ago. Said you'd glance it over, you know, er—

HARRIS. Oh, ah, yes, *Prince Claude; or, the Castle Spectre.* I—

SHAKESPEARE (*apologetically*). *Hamlet; or, the Prince of Denmark*, I think I—

HARRIS. Oh yes, so it was. Yes, very pretty thing; nothing much in it though—undramatic—hardly the thing to suit us.

SHAKESPEARE (*after a pause, speaking with a slight tremor in his voice, and smoothing his hat abstractedly, but with great care*). I—I rather thought it would have suited you. I thought it—it—you know—strong, you know, in the play scene, and at the grave; and—I, Hamlet, I thought it would have been a good part for you. Just suited your style. A good opportunity for pathos, you know, in the parting with Ophelia, and with the mother, and—

HARRIS. Oh, no, nothing in the part at all; and the speeches are too long altogether, and rambling. We want smartness, you know, my boy, in a play —everything brisk and quick. All those long-winded soliloquies, they'd kill any play.

SHAKESPEARE. I meant them as typical of the character. You see, he's a very thoughtful, moody man, and all that, and—and—they seemed to me to be—to be what a dreamy, deep-thinking, suffering man would say to himself when his brain and heart were wracked—with life, like a great, cruel wave rising to dash him down, and his puny hands are so powerless, the father that he loved lies murdered in his grave, and the woman—the sweet-loving girl!—

HARRIS (*interrupting*). Yes; well, I read it carefully through, and I didn't like it. I haven't time to argue about it. The ghost business isn't bad, but all the rest is utterly worthless.

SHAKESPEARE. Then you can't do anything with it?

HARRIS. Certainly not. (*A pause*). The thing's no good as it stands. If you like to take my advice—I'm an older man than you—you'd cut out all those long speeches, and work in a detective. Something might be done with it then, perhaps, in the provinces.

SHAKESPEARE. What, to track the King down, like?

HARRIS. Yes, I should think you might make a fair play of it then. Work up the ghost a bit more.

SHAKESPEARE (*eagerly*). Would you take it then, if I did that?

HARRIS. No. *I* couldn't. I merely threw out the idea to you, as I **know** something about these things.

SHAKESPEARE. Then it's no good, of course, my leaving it **with you any** longer (*taking it from the table and looking rather sadly at it*).

HARRIS. None, whatever, my **boy.**

SHAKESPEARE. Well, thank you **very much** for having **read it, Mr. Harris.** Good morning.

Mr. HARRIS, *absorbed in his letters, makes no response,* **and** Mr. SHAKESPEARE, *taking up his hat, and trying to fix his MS. under his coat* **so that it won't be seen,** *goes out, closing the door softly behind him.*

CHAPTER IV.

" PLANTING."

AND now the play—the sparkling comedy, the exciting drama, the screaming farce—is written, and has been neatly " typed " or copied out. Always see to this most carefully. The play must be easily readable or it won't be read, or if it be read, read with growing irritation and perplexity, not conducive to its chances of acceptance. To have it "typed " is the most practicable. Type-writing is nearly as plain as printing, and very cheap—cheaper than " copying " indeed. Mr. Gilbert had his first play printed, I know (there are few people who don't know that fact by this time, I should think), and Mr. Gilbert showed himself, thereby, wise in his generation. But then that was the last but one generation, and before the days of Remingtons and Columbias, or he would not have paid seven or eight pounds for printing, when he could have had it typed for five to ten shillings an act. I am not going to advertise any particular type-writing firm. There are five or six of them in the neighbourhood of the Strand, and one is much about as good as another.

Let me see, where were we? Oh yes, I remember, the play is finished and typed and ready for acting, and the only thing remaining is to get it accepted.

Well, you will naturally think, in the case of such a **piece as** this, that can't be very difficult. Managers will jump at it. **My** dear boy, you don't know them. You've no idea how blind they are to their own interests. Why I, myself—an important, clever writer like I am—have, at this moment, in my desk, plays that brilliant, startling, dramatic, **and** amusing **that** they would create quite a furore in Europe **if they** were only produced, and managers read them, and then hum and hah over them, and hesitate about them, and throw cold water upon them as though they were quite ordinary, commonplace plays. One is too farcical, and they are going to give up farces. **Another is too** serious, and they are going to give **up serious plays. That one** has no **part** for Mr. **Jones, and** this one wouldn't suit Miss Brown. And one is too long, and the public won't sit out long pieces ; and another is too short, and the public want a good deal for their money now-a-days. **And** a third the company doesn't suit, and a fourth doesn't suit the company. Besides, the manager has got too many plays on his hands already, and can't look at any more.

That is how they go on, throwing away fortunes like that.

I have sworn not to reveal professional secrets anywhere in these pages, or I could surprise you, my dear young reader, pretty considerably with the names—the very well-known names —of dramatists who must be well accustomed to the **sensation** of having their plays rejected. **It** is not exclusively beginners either in literature or stage work that are alone familiar with the dreary legends, " Returned with thanks," " Declined with compliments." By the way, did you ever hear of the young man who tried to become a contributor to one of our leading magazines ? **He** kept on sending in articles, and the editor kept on sending them back ; till **at last** he got so mad that he sent in a Latin noun ; he said he knew there wasn't an editor in England that could decline that. But this is frivoling, and these pages **are** supposed **to be** serious.

The most successful men find difficulty in getting their work accepted. Sims's *Lights of London* went round to nearly every manager in London before Mr. Wilson Barrett was 'cute enough to produce it, and, indeed, Mr. Sims had so despaired of its ever seeing the footlights that he had turned it into novel form and published it as a tale. And at the time, remember, Mr. Sims was not an unknown dramatist, but the author of three extraordinarily successful plays. *Jim the Penman* had a similar and even longer fight, though the late Sir Chas. Young was a man of much influence and wide acquaintanceship in the theatrical world. Mrs. Kendal, among others, objected to the play on account of the character of the wife. It was produced at the Haymarket, not at the risk of the management, and with very little idea on their part that it would prove anything but a failure. Tom Robertson—well "in" the magic circle at the time—walked about for I hardly like to say how many years with the MS. of *Caste* under his arm. "Too talky-talky" they all said. "No plot—no story—no complication—no good!" With your play in your pocket, my young friend, you can reckon you have three years' hard work before you in getting it played ; and your talent for writing is a useless ornament to you without the "character"—the "grit" necessary to transform your written fancy into an acted fact—without the force, as Tennyson has it, to make your merit known.

Therefore, do not despair at repulse ; do not lose your temper at delay ; do not snivel and snarl at disappointment. Go about the job (it is a big one) quietly, and in business-like manner. You will, if you deserve it, win in the end. Nature never wastes materials. "Mute Miltons" exist but in imagination—not in her solid halls of fact. If she means a man to be a poet, or a painter, or a dramatist she sees the matter through.

I cannot lay down any hard and fast rules for you to go upon in getting a play accepted. It would be like laying down hard and fast rules for getting your girl to accept you. I can only offer suggestions and hints. The **actual** details, of **course,** depend upon what sort of man you yourself are, what sort **of** man your manager is, and what the particular circumstances of the particular case may be. **For instance, one** may **say,** generally, that personal interviews **have** more effect upon managers and **actors than have letters, which, as** a rule, they never answer. But if you happen, as **is** not at all unlikely in a young literary man, to be of a painfully nervous temperament, then it will be far better for you to go about the **work by** correspondence. **Again, the** peculiar knack **of fly** throwing that would induce **one** manager **to bite** would frighten away another ; **and laying down** instructions for the different handling of each man would be useless. **The** managers of to-day are not the managers of to-morrow. To know the best mode of approaching Mrs. Bernard Beere or **Mr.** H. Beerbohm-Tree might probably enough be but small good **to you** by the time your play was ready, and to reveal to **you the** soft side of **Mr.** Wilson Barrett or Mr. Hare would not only endanger my life at **the** hands of those gentlemen ("speshul 'dition ! 'tack on dramatic horther by well-known London manager—'orrible scene—speshul ! ") but would promptly convert that soft side of theirs into their very roughest side, and I shouldn't know how to tackle them myself then when I wanted **to.** No, I can only show you the direction. You must find the path for your-self.

First of **all, however,** following the true bucolic method, I will point **out to you** the way *not* to go. You know the sort of thing I mean. You meet a country bumpkin, and ask him the way to Podger-in-the-Hole, **and** he scratches his head, and turns round three times, and then points along the road and tells you to go straight on, and about a mile and a-half you'll come across a lane, leading off to the left by a haystack. " Leading off to the left by a haystack," you repeat, " Yes ? "

Yees, weel, doan't 'ee gaw down theer," he replies, at the rate

of three words a minute, " 'cause that don't lead naweer. But
'ee keep straint oan and ee'll come to a stoil." " A stile," you
say, beginning to get rather impatient, " Yes, well." " Yees, an
as I wor sayin' 'ee cooms to a stoile. But 'ee mustn't gaw
oveer that, ee knaw, cause that be only the way ta Farmeer
Wurzles's," and so on.

In the same way, I say to you, don't make yourself a
nuisance. Don't hang about the stage door or other spots,
lying in wait for the manager, till he gets to dread the sound of
your name. Don't write him long and excited letters three
times a week. Don't make pitiful appeals to him on sentimental grounds. Mr. Wilson Barrett, when playing Chatterton,
was attacked with great energy by a young gentleman to the
tune of:—" Ah, you can rave about the sorrows and trials of
a young author in imagination. You can enter into his feelings
well enough upon the stage ; but you will not put yourself out
of the way to help one in real life." That was not business.
Even if you do feel yourself slighted and ill-used, you should
not show it. Put your lips tight together, and bear it.

Don't ever send in a play without first having obtained permission to do so. Don't, when it is in, worry the manager
about it too soon or too often. Don't write to the papers about
your ill-treatment. They will insert your letter, and, at the
same time, write a leader pointing out what ill-regulated, foolish
persons you and your class are, and you will get your name up
as a quarrelsome party who should be avoided. Do not argue
with managers, but accept their decisions, and appear to be
impressed with, and grateful for, their views. If they think
your play stupid, your opposition will never make them think
it is not stupid, but your agreement will make them think *you*
remarkably clever. Don't be satirical. I know you are. All
we clever men are. But it is a dangerous gift, as the young
lady said who was so beautiful that the monkey would kiss her,
and you should dissemble it. Be guided by common sense in

your tactics. Do not send drawing-room comedy to the Adelphi, and sensational melodrama to Terry's. Do not try to talk Mr. Toole over into playing **a** heavy, emotional drama, because you will only be wasting your own valuable time, to say nothing **of** that versatile comedian's. Do not send a farcical comedy to Drury Lane, or submit **a** piece containing a wreck at sea, a dynamite explosion, view of Constantinople, and vivid representation of the Jubilee procession to the **Strand** or Royalty Theatres. **Do not offer a one-act** farce **as curtain-raiser to a** house that is playing **a three-act one as its chief attraction, nor** send a **pathetic little** drama of *The Step Sister* type **to the** Gaiety.

Send one-part plays to the actors or actresses that they would best suit. **Actors are** more get-at-able than managers, and if they **fancy** the part they may push the piece for you, and of course they have naturally much influence (more of this anon). *The Red Lamp*, I am thinking, would have **stood a** very poor chance of production if sent **to** Messrs. Russell and Bashford instead of to Mr. Tree ; and **Mr.** Irving would hardly have bought *The Amber Heart* if it had not **been for** Miss Terry. Every actor and actress, especially young rising **actors** and actresses, are ever on the look-out for plays in which they themselves particularly shine, and if you can write a piece containing a part just adapted to their style, and calculated to afford them a good "display," that piece stands a very good chance of being very carefully considered. Such plays—one-part plays— are, in consequence, the best line for a beginner to work. Mind, however, that the play *is* a one-part play ; actors do not relish rivalry. And take care that the parts suit your man all through. It is popularly supposed that **an** actor can represent any character—that Toole could easily play Hamlet, and that **for** Mr. Penley to impersonate Henry VIII. would be merely a question of making-up. Actors themselves, though, know that this is not so, and that their range extends only to the bounds of their own personality. The **part in** which an actor shows himself at his **best is** that part in which his own private individual characteristics are displayed to their most dramatic **advantage.** The poorest actor, given the necessary technical training, **can act one** character **to** perfection, that character **being** himself, **while the greatest performer is stagey** and artificial **when once outside his own nature.**

See, however, **that the part fits your actor thoroughly,** and **that** it is nowhere **beyond his powers; if it is, he will tell you** that it is an impossible character, **and contrary to the laws of** human nature.

All this, too, will be excellent practice in preparing **you for the** time **when you will have to " write to** order," to fit **a** company,' as the term goes. **What a** hideous necessity having to do that is, by the **way.** It is like making a **man to** fit some **old** coat and trousers that the tailor **happens to have** on hand, and doesn't **know what to** do with. **How can the critics expect** art and drama when **a manager's instructions to** a struggling author are—if not in words, **in very plain meaning—"Oh,** play be **damned! See** that the girl **and I get plenty of** fat; that's all **that's wanted"** And, **the author—but there,** who cares for the **author?** It is the actor, in his flaring costume, that poses in graceful attitudes on the top **of the** pole for the people to gape at. The author **is the party who puffs about** underneath, supporting the pole **on his chest. Nobody** looks at **him.**

Adopting this course—this **course of** writing plays **that you** will send to actors in **the** first instance rather than to **managers** —**will gain you acquaintanceship** with **players, and such an** acquaintanceship is, remember, **your chiefest aim, object, and goal.** It is by actors' help principally that you will get a footing in the theatrical world. **You must, somehow, by** hook or by **crook, by fair means or by foul, secure** the friendship of one or **more actors—the more the better. Without** them your case is **hopeless. Few managers will be** found to pay any serious attention to the work of men unknown to them. I should say no manager ever does so, but that I have heard from the lips of some most positive assurances that **they** do I should not otherwise have believed it.

But anyhow, **and** even if **any of** them do pay attention **to** unknown men, men **known** to them **by** some **means or** other stand a much better chance of their favour, and the introduction will come with more weight from an actor than **from** any **other** person. Added to this, your **actor friend** knows how, when, and where, and with what bait your manager should be fished. **He** knows the **general** habits **of the** creature, **its shy season, its** hungry times, its particular taste. **It** is but little **use** getting a manager to **read a play when he is** not actually wanting a play ; he will have forgotten all **about it by the** time he is. While a play is drawing, it never seems to occur to them that it will ever cease to draw, and they rarely trouble themselves about **its** successor until they are dropping £100 or so a week over it.

You do not know the ground. You waste your time **on** the **wrong** trail, and chances go by while you are following up false **scents.** What you want is a little note one morning : —

" DEAR——

" Have you anything that would do for us ? Pinero's piece has fallen through, and Thorne's off his head for a play. Wouldn't that last thing of yours do—that four act one? Write the old man up a bit for T. T. Run down to the theatre and see him this morning ; you'll catch him between 11 and 12. I'll speak to him about it meanwhile.

" **In haste, yours,**——."

Then, when you go down, instead of **the stage-door** keeper coming back with a message that Mr. Thorne is very busy, and will you see Mr. Alport, you will at once be asked to "Step this way, please, and mind the stair."

An actor can be of immense service to **you at the** beginning of your career (as you can be to him when you are once an established author). He has the ear of the manager, and can speak the right word for you at the right moment. He is standing at the wings, and the piece, which has had a long and successful run, is going a little dull. The house is not so full as it hitherto has been, and the applause is sounding weaker. The manager strolls thoughtfully forward, and stands watching the stage.

" Not going so well to-night," says your friend the actor.

" No," says the manager, dreamily.

" We shall want a change soon."

" 'Fraid so."   (A pause.)

" Heard a lovely play read the other day."

" Oh ! "

" Yes ; just the thing for you—some splendid scenes in it. '

" Who's it by ? "

" There's one situation in the third act, the finest thing I've ever come across.   Splendidly worked up, too."

" Who's the author ? "

" Full of interest, beautifully written, not a——"

" Is it your own ? "

" No ; a friend of mine, a very clever young fellow   He's got the real stuff in him."

" Ah ! I never care much about venturing upon an untried man— too risky."

" Oh, he won't be untried long.   This piece is coming on soon. I think the Macklins have got it. They were wanting it I know." (This is a lie.)

" Got good parts for Brown and Robinson ? "

" Oh, there's a part in for Brown that would simply make the success of the piece without anything else ; and there's a delightful part for Robinson, too.   Oh, it really is—I don't say it because he's a friend of mine—but it really is a damned fine play."

" Well, tell him to send it down. I'd like to have a **look at** it."

" Well, **I** can't say; **I** think, as I said, he's parted with **it** already; I'm not sure."

" Can you find out, and let me know ? "

" Well, look here, I'll tell you what I'll do, if he *hasn't* settled —I don't expect he has finally yet—I'll send him down to you to-morrow."

" Very well, I shall be here about eleven, **and if he** comes we can talk it **over."**

So you go down at eleven, and talk it over, and try **to** persuade him that it **is** the grandest play that was ever **written, and to** convey to him some slight conception of its brilliancy, **its** power, **its** novelty, **and its** exceptional suitability in every direction.

In his interests, and merely as **a friend,** you advise **him,** strongly, not to let the chance slip by him of securing the piece. You hint, vaguely, concerning the anxiety of other managers **to** get hold of it—only you want him to hear it first. You expatiate —if he is an actor—upon the splendid **part there is** in it for himself, a part, too, which he alone can do full justice to ; and you talk to him of the ease with which it can be produced, and the ridiculously small expense required for " putting it on." Then you prove to him, conclusively, that it is bound to be **a** success ; **and** exemplify to him **that it is just the** sort of piece the public want. If, for instance, it is a farcical comedy, you dwell upon the fact that farcical comedy is the only thing that " draws " now-a-days. If it is not **a** farcical comedy, you explain that farcical comedy is played out, that playgoers are sick of mre tomfoolery, and require sense and wit. If it is a melodrama you bring forward the whole history **of** the stage to show that melodrama always has been, and always is, the favourite dish with the great mass of the paying public. If it is a comedy or a tragedy, you say that people are tired of the old hackneyed

D

melodramatic stuff they have always had **set** before them, and are longing for a **change.**

All of which, although not rousing him to any visible enthusiasm, **impresses** him, **and he says :**—" All right, my boy, I'll **hear it on Thursday** morning **at twelve, here** in the theatre." **And you answer : " Twelve o'clock on** Thursday—right, I'll be **down.''**

Then you shake hands and part, and till twelve o'clock on Thursday **your life moves** slowly on its wheels.

CHAPTER V.

READING.

AND now it is twelve o'clock **on** Thursday, and here we are at the stage door as the clock is striking. Ah, we shall not be quite so punctual when we are a little more familiar with the theatrical world, and know that its time is arranged on auctioneer's principles, and that twelve is for twelve-thirty o'clock precisely.

We have, it is probable, had a glass of sherry or a nip of brandy coming along, but even that has not made our knees quite as steady and our voice quite as clear as we could wish ; and there is a guilty huskiness about our manner of asking the stage doorkeeper if the manager is in, suggestive of our having come to borrow money, or sell him a dog.

He is a slightly gruffy party, the stage doorkeeper, and a little hard of hearing. He rises and comes towards us with his newspaper in his hand, and we repeat our question. He regards us with great suspicion, and says no, the manager isn't there, his tone implying that it is the last place in the world where any sensible man would expect to find him. We remark "Oh!" upon this, and look round vacantly. Then Cerberus asks us if we have any appointment with the manager, and on our eagerly responding in the affirmative, he says, "Wait a bit," and pulls open the inner door, and calls out for Harry. Harry, an intelligent lad—call boy, errand boy—emerges, whistling, with an empty beer can in his hand, and to him Cerberus appeals as to the probability of the manager's coming or not coming. Harry knows all about the matter, and expects the manager any minute, and if you are Mr. Blank (you are Mr. Blank) you are to go down stairs and wait for him. So down you go.

The inside of a theatre is a dismal place by daylight. The empty stage is dimly lighted by one flaring gas jet issuing from an upright T in the centre of the footlights. A shadowy figure in a white jacket is hovering about at the back, hauling "wings" and "flats" about, and carrying on a conversation with an unseen "Bill," whose answers appear to come from high up, or low down, you can't tell which. But it all seems very ghostly. The curtain is up, and the house looks small and dingy. The stalls and decorations are shrouded in dirty white cloths. The sunshine streams in here and there, and makes the place look still more dreary. You walk about, and get the hump.

Every step you hear, and the banging of every door, you fancy is the manager coming, and you rush to the stairs to see. You wonder if he has come and doesn't know you are there. You wonder if he has forgotten the appointment. You wonder if anything has happened to him.

At last! after waiting about half an hour (don't be too surprised though if he doesn't turn up at all. I said in a previous chapter that a theatre was a house of business, and so it is, but the folks in connection with it might be more business-like for all that. Some of them are, in our idiomatic language of Cockaigne, fair cough-drops). In the present case, we suppose that our man is a tolerably well-behaved member of his class, and, as I was saying, he, after half an hour or so, arrives, accompanied by his stage-manager, and the three of you then

proceed to either the great man's own private sanctum, or **else**
to the green-room, and the business of the day begins.

It is a trying ordeal, under any circumstances, the reading of
a play ; and listening to one is just fifty times worse. I never
could have believed what a terrible punishment hearing a play
read was until some two years ago, when one was read for **the**
first time to me. We started at seven o'clock in the evening,
all as jolly as sandboys (I haven't the ghost **of a** notion what a
sandboy is, or why it should be jolly ; but it's a good **old** well-
established simile, **and I always** use it when I **get a** chance.
My poor father was fond of it too, I remember. **It has** always
been a favourite with our family). Yes, as jolly then as
sand boys **we** were at seven—two of us to listen and one to
read. " Go it, **old** man," we said ; and he coughed, **and**
went **it.**

We laughed at all the jokes in the first act, and criticised the
characters, and argued about the plot, and said we thought it
very good. **The** second act began at nine. **We** discussed it
less at detail. The jokes in that act were not so good ; the
interest in the story was not so absorbing as it had been.
I and the **rest** of the audience **got** into a sort of habit of
looking somewhat frequently at our watches, and shaking
them to see if they had stopped. **I** and **the** rest of
the audience agreed, at the end of the act, that the play
was still very good, but that it would want cutting. On
the author, however, showing an inclination to argue the point,
we gave in, and agreed that it didn't want cutting, and begged
him to get on with the third act. The reading of the third act
commenced at 10.35 ; at 10.40 the rest of the audience wanted
to know what time the last train left for Battersea. Why,
seeing that he resided in the next street but two, he wanted the
last train to Battersea, I have never been able to understand. I
said I believed it went at 11.55. But he said no ; he thought it
was 10.50, and, murmuring something about its being a matter

of life or death, and having **only just** recollected it, he left without another word.

So I listened to the remainder of the play by myself, but what it **was about** I couldn't tell you to save my life. Whether **the hero married the heroine, and who turned** out to be the rightful heir, I don't know—and I didn't care. Somebody died about the middle **of the act, and I was glad of it. That** is all I recollect, most of my energies **having been** concentrated at **the time upon my endeavours to yawn without opening my** mouth. It **is** a difficult and exhausting feat. **You** swell inwardly, your nostrils dilate, your lips **and eyebrows are compressed, and give you a vicious, murderous** appearance. At last the water comes into your eyes, and you breathe hard, and it is over. **And then the** whole process immediately commences again.

And yet it was a **very** good play, and, when it came out about nine months afterwards, **proved a smart and rattling** piece **enough.**

That experience taught me **two useful lessons.** One was not to ever **read a play to** anybody **except as a** matter of painful necessity, and, in the interests **of** your friends, I strongly recommend the rule to you. Very **young authors** rather fancy they are conferring a favour in giving their fellow-mortals an opportunity of listening to their compositions, **but I can assure you** the fellow-mortals do not regard it in any festive light at all. **It** only bores them, and their manner shows this, whatever their conventional gush **may say; and then the** young author is **in the** depths of despair, **and loses all belief in himself** and his **work.** Don't worry your friends at all about your work. You don't really want their opinion; **you only** want their praise. They know this, and tell you that the piece is lovely—the finest **thing they** have ever heard—will be **sure to make** a great success—no difficulty about getting *that* **out,** they should think, etc., etc.—but : **"never had such** a fearful four hours in all my life " is what they say to each other when they get outside. **If** they do express their views honestly—give you " their candid opinion," as you have begged of them—it will in nine cases out of ten be to tell you that they do not like it, and that will upset you and do no good. To attempt to follow their sugges- tions would be to expose your play to the fate of **the old man's** donkey. You must judge your work for yourself, and rely upon your *own* opinion. Especially, above all things, **do** not ask another literary man *his* views about **it**. **Each** artist looks at his art from his own platform. He cannot see it from a brother artist's standpoint, and consequently all work **but his** own, how- ever perfect it may be, must of necessity appear distorted to his eyes. Shakespeare's **work** seems to **me** in many ways to be false and faulty ; and were Shakespeare alive, he would, I am convinced, object to **my methods**. **Thus do artists** disagree.

The second lesson that I learned by that **reading** was not to despair when other people yawned and dozed while listening to the reading of a piece of mine. A play is written to be acted, not read, and that it does not sound exciting at the desk is no proof that it will be dull when on the stage. Besides, I doubt whether listening to some two or three steady hours' reading of the best novel or tale—things which are written for reading— would prove exhilarating. I shouldn't care to sit out a whole morning of even " Middlemarch."

But we are wandering away from the little room where the manager and the stage-manager are waiting to hear our play. Let us **return** there and read it.

It will, as I say, be a trying ordeal for you. It will always be so, right up to the end of your career.

If you are a young author, full of hope and belief in your- self, and with corresponding capacity for disappointment and despair, the strain is pretty well as much as you can bear. When you are an old one, with your reputation, not to make, but—far more difficult—to maintain, and when managerial confidence in you, once shaken, would be impossible to re-establish, the tension is even still more severe.

The room is cold and cheerless, and you feel that your two companions and yourself make but a poor show in it. The manager is opening and reading his letters in an abstracted manner, and appears to have forgotten who you are, and to be fitfully wondering why you are there, and why he is there, and what it is all about. As for the stage-manager, he makes no attempt to disguise his opinion that the whole proceeding is a piece of foolishness ; and before the reading commences you have come to view the thing in the same light yourself, and to wish that you were the proprietor of a prosperous fried fish shop, and had never bothered your head about plays at all.

Then the manager requests you to "Fire away," and you sit down and open your MS., and begin.

Much depends upon how you read. A poor play can be given the semblance of sparkle and wit by a clever reader, but authors, generally speaking, are not good readers—F. C. Burnand and W. S. Gilbert being the exceptions that only prove the rule— and more often a piece with real humour and "go" in it will sound flat, stale, and unprofitable to the two weary listeners who form its first audience. Also, it is difficult to read with any spirit at all under the circumstances. A crowd of two is not an invigorating one to perform before, even when both are sympathetic and admiring, and to interest or amuse a manager or stage-manager in any play is like trying to excite a newspaper editor about politics. They have heard plays till they are sick of the very word play. They know all your jokes by heart. They have been familiar with all your novel situations for years, They can tell you the whole of your plot after hearing the first fifty lines. The speeches at which you have pictured the whole house rising with enthusiasm they sit through unmoved, only remarking at the end that it will want cutting; and the humour that you have feared would be almost dangerous as likely to send weak persons into too severe convulsions, **they sit and stare at** with fixed, glassy eye.

And yet you can very soon tell **if** the piece is " going " with them. They do not laugh, they do not smile, they **do not say** anything. There is no outward sign whatever **from** which you can gather any opinion. But an intangible, undefinable, **electric** current seems to run round from **one to the other, and you** *feel* that they are in sympathy with **you, and** that you are carrying them with you as you read.

Sometimes a startlingly strong **and novel** piece will work them up to such a degree that they actually *show* emotion. If the manager titters upon the first or second witty line, and goes on to laugh heartily as you turn over the pages, you can begin to think about the terms that you will ask. I have heard tell of an instance in which the stage-manager was observed to wipe away a tear during the reading of the pathetic part of **a play.** If so, the situation must have been **wondrously sad. I rather** doubt the whole story though myself.

To read on against a strengthening conviction that your labour is useless, that they do **not care** for **the piece, and are sure** not **to** accept it, **is** terribly depressing work. The silence of the room, broken only by the sound of your own voice, grows more oppressive every moment. The air seems to get colder. You go **on** grinding out the lines in a dull, hopeless, mechanical manner. You have no sense of what you are reading, and you give no sense to the words. Your throat is dry and parched. You **try** to rouse yourself up, to throw some fire into your reading, but it is useless. The deadness only deepens, and you feel as thankful as the other two, when at last it is all over, and the manager has thanked you for giving him the pleasure of hearing the piece, and you have thanked the manager for giving you the pleasure of reading it to him, and you are outside in the open air and can breathe.

When, on the other hand, however, it is plain that your

manager is enjoying the play more and more as it goes on, and his acceptance of it appears more and more certain every moment, then your reading becomes almost ecstatic. You rattle through the comic scenes with unctuous gusto, and the manager laughs and shakes in his seat, and the stage-manager gravely guffaws. The heroine recounts her woes, and your voice quavers with emotion, and the manager blows his nose, and the stage-manager quietly sighs and looks at his boots. Your hero thunders forth his magnificent defiance of the villain, and the room resounds with your passionate tones, and the manager's eye fires, and his fist clenches in sympathy, and the stage-manager shakes his head and looks determined. And when you have finished, the manager jumps up and turns to the stage-manager with—" Well, I think that's the sort of thing we want, isn't it ? " and the stage-manager, though less enthusiastic in his manner, smiles, and says that he thinks they can do with it.

After that, terms are discussed. (These not being quite so brilliant for the author as is generally supposed. But of this more anon); and, when they are settled, the " casting " is argued out, and arranged.

" Well, Annie Hughes will play Maria, I suppose,' says the manager, turning to the stage-manager.

" Isn't she rather affected ? " says the stage-manager.

The stage-manager never likes anybody's acting, and makes a virtue of always speaking his mind.

" Ah, how charming she was in that thing 'of Rae's at the Criterion," murmurs the manager, thoughtfully.

" I think she's all right," strikes in the author, " if she's kept well in hand."

" Ah, that's all very well to say, but will you keep her well in hand ? " replies the stage-manager ; " I don't care for the job, I tell you frankly."

" I think that **will** be all right, Tom," says the manager. " She must understand that she's not to play about **in it.**"

" Oh, very well. We can but try."

Maria—Annie Hughes.

" Who'll play Angelina **?** "

" You won't **better** Cissy **Grahame for that," says** the stage-manager.

" We wan't someone very strong **for that,"** puts in the author, anxiously. " That's **the part I'm more nervous about** than any."

" Well, my dear boy, you couldn't want anyone **stronger.** She's been doing some very good work lately, Cissy has." **(The** stage-manager always regards himself as a permanent opposition. If the author or the manager fancy anyone, he regards that person as **a duffer. If they** are doubtful of anyone, he **is** that person's champion.)

" Oh, all right, as long as you are satisfied about her strength. I don't remember her in anything, myself, lately."

" Oh, you'll find her all right," adds the manager assuringly. Angelina—Cissy **Grahame.**

" Now, what about Granthorne ? " asks the **author.**

" Yes, that's our difficulty," remarks the manager.

" You'll have to engage **someone for** that," says his lieutenant. The three people stare **at one another** for a bit, and ponder.

" What do you think of Bassett Roe ? " suggests **the** opposition.

" Hardly his style," replies the governor. **Besides,** he'll only play villains now, I know."

" Lewis Waller has been coming to the front **a** good deal lately," is the second suggestion of the stage-manager.

" H'm," says the author. " Think he'd do ? "

" It is a most difficult thing to put your hands on a **good** juvenile lead nowadays," parenthetically observes the chief.

" How do you like Waring ? " hazards the **author.**

"He'd do all right, but we can't get him."

"Cartwright," suddenly exclaims the author, as if he'd just guessed a riddle.

"Not your man at all," says the stage-manager.

"What would he want?" asks the manager.

"Oh, you'd get him for ten."

"Nearer twenty," says the opposition.

"Well, say fifteen," says the author gaily, who, not having to pay, looks upon this arguing about five or ten pounds a week as foolish.

"Bucklaw," says the manager, musingly.

"Bucklaw's your man," says the other; "and you'd get him for about ten or twelve."

"Do you think he could do it?" inquires the author.

"Well, he's been playing all Wilson Barrett's parts in the provinces. He ought to."

"Bucklaw, Bucklaw," mutters the author, "wasn't that the man at the Opera Comique?"

"Yes—he played the lover—the young Scotchman."

"Oh, yes—Oh, he'd do splendidly."

"I wonder if he's free?"

"Soon find out."

"Well, we'll take it that he is for the present."

Granthorne—Bucklaw.

And so on, and so on, till the casting is complete. Then the manager, saying he will write and let you know when the reading before the company is fixed for, shakes hands and wishes you good morning; and leaving the MS. on his table, you go out much easier in your mind than you came in.

The dingy little street is a radiant road, the London air is sweet and pleasant in your nostrils. The dirty urchins round about are your brothers, and you love them all. You love everybody. Even your wife's relations you do not positively dislike, for the moment.

CHAPTER VI.

MATINÉES.

I LEFT you at the end of the last chapter in a very happy frame of mind indeed. You had read your play to a manager, and it had been accepted then and there, terms settled, and cast arranged. Three days afterwards an envelope arrives, bearing the name of the theatre and its lessee printed very prominently across it. This you naturally guess to be an appointment for the reading before the company, and, trembling with suppressed delight, you break the seal. The letter expresses shortly the manager's regret that circumstances have arisen rendering it impossible for him to produce your play as arranged, the MS. of which he returns by book post ; and you sit down in the nearest chair, and stare round you vacantly, and wonder why your mouth is getting so dry.

You pull yourself together, however, in a day or two, and, finding it impossible to get your first man to reconsider his decision, set to work to get another home for the piece. You see or write to pretty well every manager in London, and a few country ones besides. To some of them you read it, and they don't care for it, as it doesn't suit them—do not always attribute a manager's declining a piece to his not liking it. Of course: " I like it very much indeed, my boy ; but I couldn't use it just at present," is, as a rule, the polite formula for "Your play is utter rubbish, my dear fellow, and I wouldn't have it as a gift." But occasionally a man really likes a piece, and yet does not see his way to accepting it. It does not fit in with his company, or his theatre, or his stage, or his pocket, and he has regretfully to let it go. To other managers you have sent it for them to read themselves, and it has come back, in one or two instances, by the next post almost, which has greatly irritated you ; and in more instances not for two or three months, which has caused you still greater irritation. And you have grown to almost hate the sight of the thing, and yet, by strange perversity, to firmer and firmer believe in it, and to love it. You rail at all the managers, and call them fools, and you have grand bursts of defiance ot things in general, during which you pace your bedroom in heroic style, and shake your fist at the world, and run your fingers through your hair, and fling it back from your forehead in quite a leonine manner, and throw your arms up towards the ceiling, after Ajax defying the lightning method ; and stupid, brainless, soulless mankind *shall* have your play. You will *force* their dull eyes to see its beauties, their doltish ears to hear its music. Their sluggish hearts shall beat quick at its magic touch, and their unwilling voices swell a chorus to its praise.

You will produce it at a *matinée !*

You are quite right, but do not, let me beg of you, think of a *matinée* until you have exhausted every other means. The scenery and properties provided at *matinées* are of themselves enough to make any piece ridiculous, and the audience—well, the audience is a "deadhead" audience, and a more depressing audience to play to than a deadhead audience you wouldn't get built for you anywhere in the world. I don't know why it is ; they mean well, they applaud liberally, they look nice, but they are not, as an audience, a success, and, for my own part, I should consider a house of "first-night wreckers," who had previously been kept outside in the pouring rain for two hours, and afterwards made to sit out *No. One Round the Corner* or *Turn Him Out*, as far preferable. There is an air of unsubstantialness about a *matinée* audience. Playing to them is like playing before your own relatives; you feel they are not *real*.

Then the critics, whether they know it **or not** themselves, come prejudiced against the whole show. **It** is impossible that they can help doing so. I **have been a critic,** and **I know** what it is like **to go** four times **or so a week, to sit out, in a** stuffy theatre on a sweltering afternoon, a play which, in nineteen cases out of twenty, is utter trash. The critic, **as a rule, gets paid a** fixed salary per annum. He gets no more pay for attending and writing about a dozen pieces than he would for attending and writing about one, and all that *matinées* bring him in therefore, is more boredness and more work. Some of them, **the** pressmen, look in only **for** an act or so, getting thereby a most hazy notion **of** the plot, and then going home and criticising the play as being ununderstandable. The **great** majority of them, however, do most conscientiously sit out *matinée* after **matinée,** from the beginning of the first act to the end of the last. How they bear it I never can comprehend; they must have iron constitutions and the patience of Job. But you can't expect that they should go to one with any feelings of love and gratitude to its promoter.

The mere fact of its being a *matinée* is, by the law of averages, presumptive evidence that it will prove a failure. About a hundred new pieces are produced at *matinées* every year. Of that hundred some two are not utterly useless. The other ninety-eight never see the light again. The very word *matinée* at once conjures up visions of dreary horror; of wild, incomprehensible plots; of unconnected, meaningless scenes; of hackneyed, impossible characters; of dialogue bald as a two-year-old doll; of ancient humour, conventional sentiment, and ridiculous situations. The *matinée* is the theatrical Nazareth, and people ask one another, Can any good thing come out at a *matinée ?*

Occasionally there does. *Jim the* Penman and *The Great* Pink Pearl are two examples of exceedingly clever plays that the *matinée* has given to us, and *Wood Barrow Farm* and *Captain Swift* are still more recent samples, and yours, my youthful dramatic friend, may make another. At all events, you can but try. I put all the disadvantages and drawbacks of the system before you as a matter of duty, but these papers are not written to discourage you ; the battle is quite hard enough without that. Besides, your friends will do all that is necessary in that direction for you. For my part, if you can't get your piece accepted, and you can manage the expense, I certainly advise to bring it out in this way, rather than burn it, which is the only other thing you can do with it. It does have its chance. The press is there, and a certain number of managers and actors ; and, if there be any good in the play, and I don't see why there shouldn't be—I'm a believer in young men myself, they should be possessed of more freshness and originality, more fancy, sparkle, and fire than we old, worked-out mines—if, as I say, there be any good in the play, it will be noted.

A *matinée* will cost you, in round figures, from £100 to £120. At least that will be the outgoing. What the house may bring you in, concerning which we will talk later on, will be a set off against it. Of course, to an "insider" the expense will be much less. If you can get your theatre lent to you for nothing, and about two-thirds of your company to play for love, the thing can be done for some £40 or £50 gross. But we are not talking about "insiders," but about rank *out*siders.

I should advise you to get a good cast together. It will be a question of only about £10 or £15 on the total between a first-class company and a duffing one, and, if you can get some good,

well-known names on your bill, they will " **draw** " **more** than
their fees. Of the value to the piece of having **it** well played I
need surely not speak. To fetch down a " star " to play in your
piece is, of course, a great acquisition, but unless the part is
really an extraordinarily fine one, and, more germane to the
point still, you can induce **the** actor **to see it** in that light, you
will find this very difficult **to** accomplish. No mere monetary
consideration will induce a man, earning a salary **of £30 or** £40
a week, to devote time and labour upon a part which can bring
him no further reputation, but, on the contrary, perhaps damage
that which he already possesses, added to which, **an** important
actor does not naturally care to make himself too common.
Occasionally, however, to try, or rather to show, their strength
in a new line, a Geo. Giddens or a Fred Leslie, or even perhaps
an Ellen Terry, will play a character they particularly fancy,
and of the advantage to the author of such **a** stroke of luck **the**
history of *The Amber Heart* speaks all that can be said.

But, as a rule, it is from the ranks **of** the young, " **the**
promising" "the rising," that your recruiting takes place.
They, generally speaking, are eager to play **for you.** In these
days of long runs young actors and actresses pine for practice
and opportunity—as the formation among them of the Dramatic
Students' Society amply proves—and *matinées* afford them the
only means of obtaining these.

You will get first-class artistes of this latter kind for a **fee** of
about **five** guineas—always employ guineas in dealing with
professional folk. There **is** a difference of a shilling between a
guinea and a pound in actual value, but the difference from a
sentimental point of view it would be difficult to estimate. A
doctor who would be pleased **at a** guinea would be insulted at a
pound. If a publisher sends me a cheque for ten pounds ten
shillings for an article, I am happy ; if he sends me a ten pound
note I talk about the discourtesy with which genius is treated
by vulgar upstart tradesmen. You would get very good people

E

for five guineas. **Your second grade** characters you would get competently **played for about** three guineas ; **and your** small parts for a **guinea and a-half.** Any big person, such **as** Lottie Venne—big, speaking **artistically, I** mean—Mackintosh, Pateman, &c., I expect you would have to pay ten or fifteen to. Of course, this is speaking roundly ; the **exact** figures in each case would be a matter of arrangement at the time, and depend upon the actor's anxiety or disinclination to play, his or her degree of popularity at the time, and the nature of the part. **For the very** trying character **of Count Freund, in Percy** Lynwood **and Mark** Ambient's *Christina*, **Mr. Herman Vezin was,** I am **told, paid** £40.

You will not find the casting all plain sailing, even if you are one of those lucky beings to whom the monetary question will be of no importance. Some of the people you may want will not care for their parts. One girl won't play second fiddle to " that empty-headed little idiot " the other girl. One will make it a *sine quâ non* that the part is one in which he can wear evening dress, and another will want to know " if the sympathies of the audience are with him in the part " ; and Miss —— doesn't choose to play with that selfish brute —— ; and Mr. —— can't be expected to act, and won't, if " Miss —— doesn't play up " to him.

Others will be under engagement to various managers who will not let them play for *matinées*. Mr. Irving never, as a rule, allows any member of his company to act outside the Lyceum ; and Mr. Chas. Wyndham also has a strong objection to loaning an actor. That their manager will not let them play is, by-the-way, the excuse that artistes generally rely upon when they do not want to play. It is often the polite form of saying " I don't want to have anything to do with the piece at all," so do not, when met with this rejoinder, argue the matter, and offer to go and see the manager about it.

When you have got your company together you can fix the

date. Some of them will be playing for other *matinées*, and some will have important rehearsals at their own theatres. You must manage to select a day that will suit them all. Then also you must be careful not to clash **with** any other *matinée*, or, indeed, with **any** other theatrical **event of any kind.** Sapte's *Uncle's Ghost*, I remember, came out **on the same day as** the Mansion House lunch to the theatrical profession. **The** critics were called both by duty and pleasure rather to **the** substantial fare provided by the Lord Mayor than to the ghostly entertainment of Mr Sapte, and the next morning's notices **were few** and far between.

As regards the period **of** year, try and arrange your production early—before critics, managers, and the public have become sick of the mere word *matinée*—before the theatre is as stifling as an oven, and everyone is longing to be outside in the glorious sunshine. **In June and** July *matinées* literally swarm, and it is next to **impossible** to get a free date, and difficult to **get a cast** together. Get your play finished early. If it is not ready before the end of April far better practise patience, and leave it over till the next season.

Now, for a theatre. **This** will cost you from £20 to £35. Don't, if you can possibly help **it, ever have** anything to do with "unlucky" houses. **I** never was the slightest superstitious until **I** came to have to **do** with theatres. But, from some houses, it really does seem impossible to exorcise the demon of misfortune. The price asked should include the services of the whole of the theatre staff, both back and front—but not, of course, the use of the courteous and magnificent-looking acting manager, **to** whom you will have to pay **a fee** of from five to ten guineas. The carpenters, scene-shifters, gas men, and others behind will expect a tip, say a pound or thirty shillings given to the head carpenter to divide among the lot. The price also includes gas, programmes, band (in most cases), and the use of all scenery and properties that the house may have in stock.

E 2

You will have some rare fun over the scenery and mounting. At some of the theatres they seem to possess only one interior and one exterior. Juliet's bed-chamber on Monday becomes the Widow Melnotte's cottage on Tuesday, a pawn-shop on Wednesday, a palace on Thursday, and a boat-house on Friday. Othello and Sir Charles Surface stretch their legs under the same table, and both sit in Austrian bent-wood chairs, while " Street in Venice by Night," " Outside the Pot and Whistle, Drury-lane," and " Market Cross, St. Peter's, Yorkshire," are all represented by a " Mediæval Street." I remember " Lal " Brough getting a very hearty laugh at the expense of the —— management once (about the only thing that ever was got at the expense of that house for a *matinée*, I expect). A " comfortably-furnished apartment " in some palace or mansion was " mounted " with the usual rickety table and one chair. " Lal " apologised for this to another character in the piece, by explaining that they had " just had the brokers in."

The hire of the theatre also gives you the right to at least one full rehearsal there, with scenery, props., and music ; and as a matter of courtesy, you are generally permitted the use of the stage for your rehearsals whenever it is not otherwise employed. When it is otherwise employed you will have the enjoyment of heading your company about from one theatre to another till you find rest for the sole of your foot. Nearly any theatre is willing to lend you their stage when vacant, and you will find the acting managers most good-natured and obliging gentlemen. In the busy season, however, most of the stages are nearly constantly occupied, and then with your company trailing behind you like a school treat, you will cross from the Cri. to the Pav., or the Troc. Neither the Pav. nor the Troc are available, upon which Buggins, your leading man, who is playing at the Haymarket thinks that that house is free, and you and Buggins, leaving the others behind you, run down there to see. The Haymarket people are very sorry—pity you weren't five minutes earlier—have just lent the **stage to** Juggins and his company—think you might get in at the Adelphi. Off in a cab to the Adelphi—no good—" Tooles's, cabby." **" Yessir."** **" Oh, Mr.** Donald, **are you using your** stage this morning ?" **"** Just **this instant lent it to Muggins, or you** should **have it in** a moment." **"Dammit. Just my luck. Come on** Buggins. Princess's." " Yessir." **" Can you lend us your** stage this morning ? " " No ; **we're** using **the** stage. **Can have the** saloon if you like, though." **" Oh, can we. Thanks, awfully.** God bless you. **We'll go and fetch the gang at once."** " Trocadero, Cabby." **"Now, then, where are you all. We've** got **the Princess's saloon. Where's** Fuggins **? where's** Huggins ? **Got tired of** waiting, and **gone over to** the Criterion ? Met a friend from Australia, and gone **into Scott's,** has he ? **Ah,** we'll soon have 'em out. Miss Puggins **gone** home. Oh, **its** too bad of her, really. **Never** mind, we must **do** without her. Come on."

Your artistes will give **you** about eight **or** ten rehearsals, but two or three **of the** cast will be absent **at each,** and their parts will have to **be read.** Altogether, you **will have a** fearful time over the rehearsals, and will probably look ten years older when they are over than you did **before. I** intend to deal with rehearsals at length in my next chapter, so I will not go far into the subject here, only advising you to see that you have a good stage-manager. If you have not sufficient experience and authority yourself, it would be better to engage one, even if it does cost you seven, eight, **or ten guineas** extra. As a rule, in *matinée* rehearsals, everybody is stage-manager. This is useful, as giving liveliness to **the** proceedings, but the play suffers badly. Jones wants to arrange the thing from the point of view that the most important character in the piece is the character played by Jones. He is most indefatigable in instructing all the others how to act up to Jones, how to place themselves so that Jones is always the central figure of the picture, how to speak so that Jones's answers may be effective, how to behave so as never to take the attention of the audience away from Jones. Brown disagrees with Jones's **views** on stage management, thinks Jones too anxious to **show** his (Jones's) **part** up at the expense of the others, considers, on the contrary, that it is **Brown's part** that is the important **one** to be played **up to,** instructs the rest of the company accordingly. Rest of company disagree **from** both Jones **and** Brown, also from each other, also from **author,** whom they all think **an ass.** Result, everybody **stage-manages** everybody else, **and** complains that nobody else listens to them.

As regards the business part of your arrangements, leave these to the acting manager.

He will see to all the advertising for you, an item that will cost you about £30 or £35. Four days' advertisements in the newspapers, a dozen sandwich men (poor devils!) for a couple of days, and a few hundred posters and small bills will be all you require. Less than this will make the thing a hole-and-corner affair, and more than this is useless. You only want to attract the attention of those particularly interested in theatrical affairs. The general public it is idle whistling for.

Give him a list of your friends, and he will send them a circular, requesting their orders for tickets ; and this will save you the unpleasant task of personal touting. It will surprise you to find how many friends you have when you come to make a list of them for purposes like this. All previous little differences and dislikes are forgotten under the genial influences of such a moment, and your heart goes out to every human being whose name and address you can recollect. What if you and the man next door *have* had words over the garden wall, and you have tried to poison his cat, and he has called out across the street to his boy to come away and not be seen talking to your boy, and you have yelled out to your boy that if ever you catch him again speaking to low people's

children you'll give him what **for!** **What if** such trifles *have*
been ? Shall they be allowed **to stand in the** way of friendship
between Christian men ? **No ! you will** forgive your **enemy—**
and put his name **down.**

You are quite right, for **it is from** this list **alone that any**
actual receipts will be **brought into the** house. **One or** two
country **people,** wandering aimlessly about **the Strand** not
knowing what to do with **themselves,** may, in a **weak** moment,
turn into the pit, but **there will be no crush anywhere,** so you
must work your friends **to the last** man. **Put down** your relations even, **if you can be sure that they won't create** any
disturbance.

Your acting manager will see to the invitations to the Press
and to the managers, **and get as many** members of these **two**
classes as he can. **Actors, actresses, and** authors are admitted
on presentation of **their card.** **There is a** goodish crowd of
them always pressing round the **box-office.** Why **they come is**
a mystery.

He (the **A. M.**) **will also get your play licensed for** you.
Should you ever desire **to do this for yourself, however,** the
following is **the** course **to be adopted :—**

A neat copy of the play, bearing the signature of the
manager of the theatre at which it is to **be** presented, must be
sent, accompanied by a fee of one guinea, if in one act, and of
two guineas if in two or more acts, to " Edwin **F. S.** Pigott,
Esq., **M.A.,** Examiner of Plays, H.M. Household, St. James's
Palace." **The proposed date of production** must also be
stated. Then in **about a week, if** nothing objectionable be
found in the work, the Lord Chamberlain's license for it to be
played will be sent to the theatre. Or, if the Lord Chamberlain
does not forbid within seven clear days after the play has been
sent to him, his permission may be assumed.

Other odds and ends of expenditure will be a few pounds for
the two or three copies of the play that you will require and for

copies of the parts. Then there will be a certain amount needed for postage, messengers, tips, &c. Nothing can be done without tipping in this world; and I expect when we go to the next we shall be asked to " please remember the fireman."

That is all I can think of, and I daresay you will think it quite enough. Oh—of course if it is a "costume" play you will be expected to provide dress, wigs, &c.

If the piece is a failure, you will never hear any more of it—except, of course, from your friends. If it is a success, it will be eagerly sought for, and you will be able to command good terms. I hope it will be a success—at least, I say I hope it will, as that is the proper thing to say. As a matter of fact, I don't care a hang whether it is or not.

CHAPTER VII.

IT may be remembered that, in the last chapter, we left our hero engaged in a fearful struggle with a *matinée*. We will now retrace our steps, and return to our story at the point where the villain of this tale (the manager I mean; of course) had accepted the play, and arranged for its production. The *matinée* affair was really all a dream. Our author was very tired and sleepy when the letter of which we spoke was brought to him, and suddenly dropped off to sleep with the envelope unopened in his hand, and dreamed the events recorded. Now, however, it is morning, and he awakes and rubs his eyes. "Then that awful *matinée* was all a horrid dream," he exclaims; "and I don't owe forty-seven pounds ten shillings and ninepence, and the papers haven't said that 'another three hours' drivel was served up at the Criterion yesterday afternoon for the delectation of those unfortunate beings whom duty compels to frequent *matinée* performances.' And the letter then from the theatre, saying they were not going to do the piece after all! What! —why here it is, lying on the floor unopened? What does it say, really? 'Dear Mr. Author,—Please be down here to-morrow, Wednesday, at twelve to read *Blood Stained Bill; or,*

the Brigand of Mount Blanc to company.—Very truly yours,
T. H. E.   Manager.'"

So you see everything turned out happily after all.

At twelve o'clock he, having dressed himself in his best
clothes, and bought a new pair of gloves, coming along, presents
himself at the stage door—not hesitatingly and nervously this
time, but as if the whole place belonged to him.   Other people
—actors out of work and young authors—mere outsiders, silly,
presumptuous lads who think they can write plays, members of
" the great unacted club," poor fellows !   Our hero pities them,
but thinks it would be better if they gave up trying to force
themselves into a groove for which they are unfitted, and returned to their stools—these people are waiting about, but they
are told the manager will be unable to see anybody that morning,
as he has an important engagement.   Will our author step down
stairs into the green room ?

In the green room he finds the stage-manager talking to a
couple of gentlemen and three ladies.   The stage-manager
greets him pleasantly, and introduces him.   The gentlemen
bow, the ladies bow and smile, and our hero thinks he shall like
being a dramatic author very much.   Others soon arrive, and
everybody seems to have their best clothes on, and our hero is
glad he put his on.   Everybody is a little nervous, too, and
subdued.   Altogether, the affair is not unlike a wedding.

The manager arrives at last, and, all the company being there,
the reading at once takes place.   This is a very much more
jovial matter than was the former reading.   There is no anxiety
or doubt on either side, no up-hill fighting against chilly dis-
belief and assured boredom.   On the contrary, the company
have been told that the play is going to be a good one, and
everyone is in an encouragingly prepared-to-be-pleased mood.
They form an excellent audience, too, any company of actors
(and be it enacted that whenever " actors " are spoken of in
these papers in the masculine gender the same shall extend to

either sex), and it is a pleasure to read to them. They laugh in the right places, and become properly pensive during the **sad** situations. They **do not,** when Edwin clasps Angelina to **his** bosom with " And now, my own, my darling girl, **one last fare-** well before we part, perhaps never more to meet upon this earth," giggle behind their handkerchiefs, nor double up with a shriek, and try **to lie down** in their seats when the villain, saying " Die, then ! " murders **the good old man. They** will grasp every point. They will understand the full significance of every line. The reading is rattled through amid laughter, murmurs of delight, and even, perhaps, slight applause ; and, at the **end,** the company rise to beam smiles and congratulations upon our modest friend. Let us hope he is modest. That of itself will confer upon **him a** certain amount **of** distinction among **the** ranks of dramatic authors.

At least, this is what takes **place, provided the play is an** undoubtedly good one. **Very often, however, the** company **is** assembled to hear **a** piece **which has only been accepted** in desperation, **and because** nothing else could **be** found, **and** something must be had. Then the proceedings are by no means so smooth, and the author, especially, **has a very** rough time of it. There is depressing silence, broken **only by** coughs and fidgetings during his reading. Stoical resignation is the pervading expression of countenance, and everybody carefully avoids catching anybody else's eye. If anybody does by acci-dent do so, the look that **is** exchanged between those two is charged with a meaning which it would be difficult **to express** shortly in words. Some of the more complaining among the Psalms, together with selections from the book of Job and the Lamentations of Jeremiah would seem, though, to imply the idea. At the end, there is an ominous silence, and the audience rise, anxious to get outside and relieve their feelings by telling each other what they think of it. " Well, there you are ; that's it," says **the** manager, defiantly, and nobody contradicts him.

The author looks pale and jaded, and sits, saying nothing, till one or two have left. Then he smiles feebly and asks the stage-manager what he thinks of it. The stage-manager replies in a pre-occupied air : " Ah—well—we must see what we can do with it," and prefers to keep his opinion to himself till he finds the manager alone (the stage-manager has great influence as regards the final acceptance or refusal of a play. His voice is, indeed, the casting vote). The author, very meek and generally apologetic, then puts it in low whisper to one or two of the company what *they* think of it, whereupon they recollect that they have trains to catch, and murmuring evasive replies slide out ; upon which the author buttonholes the youngest member of the company (who is nervous and doesn't know how to get away), and proves to him that the play is an A 1 affair and bound to succeed.

Under these circumstances, the piece rarely comes to a head. The force against it is too powerful, and after floundering through one or two rehearsals, it sinks into the great quagmire of stillborn drama, and is never heard of again.

But we are not thinking of such pieces as these. We are dealing in this chapter with the brilliantly clever comedy that you, my young friend, have penned—the comedy that is welcomed by the whole company with effusion. We will even go so far as to suppose that they are all pleased with their parts, and that even the low comedy is not absolutely dissatisfied with his. Such being the case, the first rehearsal is appointed for eleven, on the next day but one, and at 11.30 on that day you will all be standing on the stage, waiting for the leading lady, who has been delayed owing to the death of a near relative.

The first few rehearsals will be mainly devoted to "positions," entrances, and exits, movements, situations, and such like. They will not become interesting from an artistic point of view until, say, after the first week, by which time the mechanic a portion of the work being fairly in hand, and "parts" having

been mastered, the " character " comes in for attention. **During**
this first week's rehearsals, however, the parts will be **read,**
heroes, heroines, villains, and comic lovers, all trapesing about
the stage with books in their hands, and gabbling through **your**
witty or poetic lines in a way calculated to break your heart.

Not that they do not **appreciate them.** No one will **do so**
more, and even in the hurry and worry of these early **times a**
frequent laugh, and a constant " What a lovely line ! " " Isn't
this a pretty scene ? " " What a splendid situation ! " tell that,
notwithstanding seeming indifference, the play is being followed
and understood.

But, of **course, as I have** said, the words and ideas are of
secondary importance just now. The " business " of the scenes
is the chief thing to be attended to.

HERO. "I love you, Anastasia, with a passion so transcendental that
neither earth, nor Heaven, nor even——." Well, now where do I take he
hand ? " At earth ? "

STAGE MANAGER. No, **no, my** boy. When you get to " Heaven."

COMIC MAN (*waiting his turn at the wings*). Never will get there. You will
arrange for it to come off at the third place mentioned, if you take my
advice.

STAGE MANAGER (*who very properly regards rehearsals from a serious point of
view—severely*). We are here to rehearse a play, Mr. ——, if you please. Not
to play the fool.

(*Comic Man unostentatiously withdraws from the scene, and is
heard no more*).

HEROINE. Well, then, am I to stand stock still all through his speech ?

STAGE MANAGER. No, no, of course not. You—what are the stage
directions ?

PROMPTER (*at table C*). " Stands proud and erect. Left Centre."

HEROINE (*laughing*). **Well, I** can't stand " proud and erect " for **five**
minutes. I shall have some gallery boy asking " if it's alive."

AUTHOR. No, no, Miss ——. You understand the idea, surely. You're
being made love to. You don't want to jump about.

STAGE MANAGER (*who has his own opinion about the author's opinions concerning these matters*). Well, my boy, she's quite right. No woman would stand
like a dummy for five or six minutes even to be made love to.

AUTHOR (*who fancies he knows all that is to be known about human nature, and*

about the habits and manners of women in particular). Well, what would she
do?

STAGE MANAGER.   Well, she'd toy with her fan or something or make some
movement towards him.

MANAGER *(who has entered during the argument, and been listening to it un-
observed, now coming forward).* How would it be to break up Laurence's
speech and let her answer him at the beginning. Then she could sit all the
while he was telling her about his mother.

STAGE MANAGER.   That's the very thing I've been arguing for all along.
You'll find you'll have to do it too when you come to see the thing worked
out.

AUTHOR.   Well, I particularly don't want to. I want that exact situation.
It will be all right you'll see when the speeches are properly given. You
can't judge of it now at all.

MANAGER.   Well, leave that now. We can easily see about it afterwards.

So, for the present, it is arranged that Anastasia is to stand
stock still while Laurence tells her about his mother, and that
he is to take her hand when he gets to " Heaven."

Every position, every movement of a hand, every fluttering
of a fan, every wink, every shrug of the shoulder is carefully
worked out at rehearsal. The distance separating a husband
and wife from each other during a quarrel is scrupulously
measured (what a pity it is not measured and maintained in
real life!), and whether Edwin's passionate kiss shall be on the
right or left side of Angelina's nose is decided by the stage-
manager's going round into the stalls, and seeing from there
which looks most full of tenderness. Grouping, posing, and
situations require an immense amount of care. That pretty
picture of Letty rushing with a little cry of joy into Robin's
arms, while her white-haired father rises, smiling, to greet him,
has cost a vast amount of labour to produce; and Letty, and
Robin, and the author, and the manager, and the stage-manager,
and the white-haired father have had a fearful time over it. The
stage-manager thought that Robin should come down c., and
that Letty should meet him there. The author, on the other
hand, would rather lose his hopes of heaven (not much of a stake

for him) than allow **that**. He **is nuts on the idea that** Robin
should stand at the door with his arms stretched out, and **that**
Letty should first exclaim " Robin !" and then run **towards him.**
Stage-manager says: **" Oh, all** right ; **do it** that way, **and you**
will spoil the whole situation." Author says, "Not at all, my
dear fellow. It will be a little novel, that's all." Letty, appealed
to on the quiet by the **author, and** not wishing to offend that
party, says she feels more like running the whole way ; appealed
to publicly **by** the stage-manager, **and** being anxious not **to**
affront that personage, says **she** does think **it would take off a**
little from the distance if Robin came down **a few steps. If the**
author is a young hand **it** is probable that **the** stage-manager's
view will be finally **adopted.** If, however, **the** former is **a man**
of standing, then it will probably be the stage-manager's views
that will suffer.

Of course, **in** the case **of** " big " authors, no one would think
of opposing their notions. A Gilbert's or a Pinero's MS. would
contain all stage directions down to the very minutest, and these
would be carried out without question.

It being at last settled where Letty and Robin are to embrace,
the white-haired father **has to be** fixed. Shall **he** rise **the**
moment **he sees** Robin, **or shall he** remain seated until **the**
lovers have done cuddling, and run towards him ? Will white-
haired father try both ways, **please,** and now the other way
again ? " Yes ; the first way is right. Will you please make a
note of that, Chudleigh ? You rise **as** Robin enters."

There will be from twenty to thirty, or even more, rehearsals
of a big piece, and after the skeleton **of** the play, as the movements **and** positions **may** be termed, has been knocked into
some **sort of** shape, the company begins to pay more heed to
the lines. Here, also, every intonation, every accent, every
laugh, every sigh is arranged, and practised, and tried again
and again, until both stage-manager and author are thoroughly
satisfied. The very big artistes naturally are left a good deal

to themselves, but the minor ones have usually merely to give effect to their instructions. On the whole, if he is under a good stage-manager, this redounds to the actor's advantage, but it must be very annoying, if, as occasionally happens, he is pitched into by the Press for doing that very thing that he himself was most anxious not to do, but which the author or the stage-manager insisted on his doing.

From all this, it will be seen that the fortunes of a play depend much upon the stage-manager, and a good stage-manager is worth his weight in £5 notes. Do not, if you are a young author, quarrel with him. He has been born and bred in the theatre, and he naturally is somewhat imbued with " theatrical " ideas, but it is better to let him have his own way than to set him against you and your piece, and he can do it far more good than he will do harm to it. Of course, I do not mean that you should give up any vital point, or suffer any change that could really injure the play. But it is not likely at all that you will come to loggerheads there. It is in small matters of detail that you will fight, and, in these, he is more likely to be right than you.

On the professional stage the great aim is to rehearse exactly as the piece will be played. Back drawing amateurs who " reserve " themselves for the evening, and like to come out with " surprises," would do well to remember that men like Irving, and Willard, and Beerbohm-Tree go through their parts morning after morning in the same tones, and with the same gestures and expressions as on the opening night. " Surprises " would not be welcomed. Everyone must know what everyone lse is going to do, and be prepared for it. Indeed, a final dress rehearsai is often a better performance of a piece than the one that fiist takes place before the public. Nothing is forgotten or bungled. There is no nervousness, no apprehension.

As the rehearsals proceed you will probably enough be required to alter your piece, to cut out one scene here and write in another one there, to shorten this part and " write up " that. If your manager is playing you may safely reckon that his part will want a lot of writing up, and you **are** lucky if it does **not** come to be a monologue. Your comic man will also want **his** part altered, **and** " strengthened " **a** good deal, **and he will** possibly offer **to help you in your reconstruction. If** there **are** *two* comic men in the piece, **God help you.**

To sum up shortly, the **period of " Rehearsals"** will be a very trying time with you, and the **business will need** all your tact. You will want to maintain and have carried **out all your** ideas, and, at the same time, not to offend the stage-manager, or differ with the manager, or quarrel with the actors. I wish you **well** of the job.

CHAPTER VIII.

PRODUCTION.

"On Saturday next will be produced an entirely new and original comedy, entitled (give it an attractive title, that is half the battle, something short, impressive, and easily remembered), written by"—well, by you, you know. Such is the announcement that appears one morning among the theatrical advertisements, an announcement which you read over a good many times to yourself with a quiet smile, though half doubting if all is not a dream. There have been so many difficulties to overcome, so many disappointments to be borne, such a long and bitter battle to fight! Over and over again have you seemed on the point of victory, and over and over again have you been driven back defeated : it seems impossible to believe that success has actually, at last, come home to you. Do not be too certain of it even then. It is just possible that in the next day's papers, when you look, you will be greeted with an advertisement stating that some revival of an old piece, or a continuation of the present one, will take the place of the production previously announced. Such things have been on more than one occasion. Of course, established and successful authors would not be played with. Men like Grundy **and Pinero would require** a written agreement, by which the manager would bind himself to produce their play within some specified time, to be entered into, before they would commence to write a play at all. But then managers have **no** wish to **break** agreements with established and successful authors. **On the** contrary, it is they, the managers, who are the parties most anxious to keep **them. A** popular author is fought after like a pretty girl at a picnic, and can dictate his own terms. **W. S.** Gilbert **used to make it a** stipulation that any play **of his—whether successful or** not— should be run for a hundred nights at least ; **and, seeing that** £200 a **week can very easily** be lost upon an unsuccessful piece, the fact that such **terms were** eagerly swallowed proves what a scarcity of good dramatic writers there must **be.**

But in the **case of** young **and** unknown authors, the boot is entirely on the **other** foot. The manager, even **if he** likes the play, has no particular **anxiety to produce it. Let us, in the** theatrical world, say what **we like, it** is an undoubted fact that there is a prejudice against new authors, merely as new authors, and quite apart from any question of their inexperience. Why managers should endeavour to narrow the market from which they draw their supply **is a** mystery which **a** business man would find it difficult **to solve,** but they themselves appear to see nothing extraordinary in such a course. Indeed, they seem more eager to maintain a dramatic "corner" than even are the members of that very corner, and I believe they would rather lose a thousand pounds over a play by an old hand than win a thousand pounds upon the work **of a** fresh man. This clannism will irritate you at the beginning of your career, but when you have once forced your way within the magic circle where it reigns, you will be loud in praise of **the** system, and indignant at any thought of interference with it.

However, when matters have gone so far that the play has actually been advertised **for** production, even a new author may, as a rule, take it that the piece is safe; and his anxiety then passes from the manager and fixes itself upon the public and the Press. I do not think you need give yourself much concern as to your first piece being a success. If a play by an unknown man has been accepted by a London manager, and has passed the various stages up to production, it is tolerably sure to be received, if not with acclamation, at all events with no disfavour; for, although how it read will be but a poor guide to how it will act, the rehearsals, as they progressed, would soon show what it would play like, and, if these rehearsals were not perfectly satisfactory, very little hesitation would be shown in giving the whole thing up.

As for the mere reading, that is never a test as to how a piece will play. A man with a vivid imagination, who concentrated all his efforts in conjuring up, as it was read to him, a complete picture of the play being performed, might be able to say decisively how anything would go; but it is very difficult to do this. Often a scene which has read delightfully plays weakly; and a piece that seems foolish when read may act quite smartly and brightly. As I said in a previous chapter, it is only *action* that can properly fill a stage, and this, to be judged of, must be seen. A narrative that would thrill us when read, sounds wearisome when two people sit R. and L. and let it off at one another across a stage. The scene between the two women, in Westland Marston's *Under Fire*, read quite excitingly; when one came to sit in a stall and *see* it one yawned. In the same way, scenes that, perhaps, read crudely and confusedly may act forcibly. The church scene in *Much Ado about Nothing* is not the same in the book as it was at the Lyceum.

Theatrical people, in particular, make very bad judges of how a play will go with the public. The artist appreciates the technique of the art. The public care about the picture as a whole. Your actor is loud in praise of the way in which a scene is built up, or a situation led to, or an acting opportunity afforded. Your public doesn't care twopence for anything so long as they are amused and interested. **To sum** up, public and artistes view a work from diametrically opposite points of view : the latter from "behind," where they see and criticise the weaving of the threads ; the **former from** "the front," where the finished fabric is seen **as** a whole, and the pattern pleases or displeases.

Now, after this little digression, we will, if you please, return to our subject, viz., the first night and its attendant circumstances.

All your **friends will, of course, expect stalls or boxes.** Well, you will have to let them expect. Nearly every booked **seat in** the house will be required for the critics, managers, **authors,** actors, and distinguished people generally, who are always invited to every theatrical event. The list numbers some two or three hundred. You will have to put your friends in the pit and gallery, where, by-the-bye, too, they will be much more **useful** to you, seeing that they will be able to applaud, and shout "Bravo," and call for "author !" there—conduct they could not pursue if in the stalls or circle. Mind, though, for goodness sake, that they don't make themselves and you (which is more important still) ridiculous over this applauding business. As a rule, the friends of the author do more on a first night to damn his play than ever he, **and** the manager, and the actors all put together do. They roar applause at everything—good, bad, and indifferent, more especially the bad and indifferent ; and that riles the people who are not friends ; and they—the people who are not friends—then tell the people who are friends to "shut up," and "go home," and "stow it" ; and there's a general **row** and riot all through. A dozen *discreet* friends (if you happen to be lucky enough to possess so large a number), who will never let it be seen that they *are* your friends ; who will only hint applause, and never persist in it if it is not taken up ; who will know the right word and the right moment to gently deprecate any opposition, and not, by boisterous abuse, to only increase it; who will laugh, when they do laugh, as if they were really amused, and not as if they were merely trying to make a noise; and who **will** express approval in the usual method, without making an exhibition of themselves—that dozen will be of far more service to you than a gross of the regulation first night "friend." **See, too, that they distribute** themselves about the house in twos and threes, not get together all in a heap.

As for yourself, you will probably have a box **into which you** will go **with** your nearest and your dearest, and **any aunt or** uncle or other person from whom **you** may have any expectations. You will sit well back in the darkest corner and listen breathlessly—not to the play **but to** the house. Will they laugh at your jokes? **Will there run round** a suppressed murmur of delight at your poetry? **a burst of applause at** your heroic sentiments? Some of your best lines **(at least,** so they are sure **to seem to** you) will be missed **out, and much of the** wit and humour you had most reckoned on will fall flat. This **will be** counterbalanced by lines you had **never thought** anything **particular** about being taken up and **applauded.**

You will not be wanted behind until the very end (if the piece **turns out a failure it** might be as well not to go even then), and you will be far better not there. The excitement and nervousness "behind" **during** a first night is something almost comical, and anybody who gets in anybody else's way there stands a very good chance of being brutally murdered, and his mangled remains put outside the stage door. I used to think that **I had** a good share of suppressed nervousness ready for most occasions, but I look upon myself as a **happy, thoughtless child on** a first night **compared with** the company. **They can't help it.** It is the acting temperament. **I have heard the** late John Clayton **—a man whom to look at,** you would not think troubled with nervousness—say that no success could ever compensate him for the agony he suffered on **a first** night.

If, however, the piece is a success you will slip out during the last act and make your way round so as to be ready for the possible and probable "call."

And now a word or two as to this call. Some folks hold that authors should never, under any circumstances, take calls, and argue that they have no business before the curtain at all, their place being the study and not the stage. But that's all nonsense. No doubt, from an artistic point of view, it is quite orrect, but there is a nature side to the question. Authors are only human (though to judge by the airs that we give ourselves you might be led to think this impossible), and they like applause. Applause, indeed, in one form or another, is what we all live for, from the statesman to the mountebank, and the sweetest form in which it can be offered us is the form that we can see and hear—the hand clappings and the cheers like the roar of the waves upon a shingly beach, the waving hats and handkerchiefs like a tossing forest before our half-dazed eyes. Very childish and little-minded it may be, perhaps, to love and long for such mere tinsel, but we men are only childish and little-minded at the best, and always shall be. Mr. Wills does, it is true, as we poor lesser lights are often reminded, rise superior to this weakness, and never appears before the curtain ; but then Mr. Wills is a philosopher of the kind you read about but very seldom meet, a man who cares more about his long clay and his glass of grog and his quiet chat than about all the theatres, and plays and playgoers, ever built. As for the average author, he, so long as reason holds a seat in his distracted brain, will be eager to take a "call."

A young author will, naturally, be especially eager to do so, and by all means let him. The only thing I have to say is, be careful that it is a genuine, unanimous call. Do not force yourself, as it were, before the curtain ; and do not go if there has been much opposition to the piece during its progress, even if you are called. If you do, you will receive what is termed a " mixed reception."

These mixed receptions are often indignantly spoken of as "author baiting," but they are really nothing of the kind, and the explanation of them is extremely simple. The pit and gallery of a theatre on a first night generally contains a certain number of " orders," who, because they are friends of the people connected with the house, or in gratitude for their free admission, can usually be reckoned upon for plenty of applause. Whether the custom is a wise one or not is a question for argument, and there is something to be said on both sides. Against the system, it may be urged that the successful houses rarely have recourse to it, and that by their indiscriminate applause the " orders," like the friends before referred to, irritate the paying portion of the audience, and create an opposition that would not otherwise arise. On the other hand, " orders " help to fill the house, and give a cheerful air to the proceedings ; while in case of success, they help to swell the approval, and, in case of opposition, they can counterbalance, or, perhaps, even drown the dissentient voices. In any event, they save the piece from being received in dead silence, which would be worse for it than any amount of row.

But I did not start to argue this matter out, but merely to explain that it is these holders of orders who are mainly responsible for the doubtful welcome that an author occasionally gets. After the curtain has finally fallen on a weak or bad play—or a play that, at all events, has not pleased the paying part of the audience—the friends and the orders, together with a few of those good, honest souls, who would applaud the tom-cat if he came and sat down on the stage, at once begin cheering and calling for " author." The regular playgoers thereupon yell out, " No, no ; we do not want the author." In spite of this, however, or because their voices are not distinguished in the hubbub, out he steps. The one section cheer vociferously. The other, as a protest against it being assumed that the play is approved of, think it their duty to howl at him as if he were a villain o the deepest dye, or belonged to the opposite political party.

Therefore, make sure, before you accept a seeming call, that it is a sure thing. You can easily forecast, during the playing of the piece, whether this will **be so or not. If your work is** not appreciated, unfavourable comments, **ironical** laughter, and occasional hisses will be **heard during the acts.**

But assuming that **the success is certain, and the call har**monious, then take it **by all means—not by rushing in before** the curtain is well **down, and** in **front of the actors : I have** seen that done, and it doesn't look at all pretty—but by stepping in modestly last **of all. Do** not appear too eager to come forward, and **do not prance up to** the middle **of** the footlights, and stand there for a couple **of** minutes, bowing and smirking like an organ-grinder on the look-out for **coppers.** This I have also seen done, and it also does not look pretty. Move two or three steps from the boxes, bow as gracefully as Nature and nervousness will permit, and **retire** promptly and quietly. Of course, you have rehearsed all this **in** the privacy of your apartment beforehand ; but you will **not** find such preparation of much use, as if, at the time, you can recollect who you are and what you are doing there it will be as much as you can manage.

If by any chance **the** play **is** a frost, and you do get hissed instead of cheered, well, you must grin and bear it. It won't kill you. It will be a hard knock for you, that is all ; and hard knocks we all have **to take** our share of in the battle of life. Cowards cry out, **and** want to lie down when they get hit ; brave **men** fight on, careless of blows. Besides, a play may fail on the first night, and yet work up into a success. *The Private Secretary* was hooted at on its first production, and " slated " next morning **by** the Press. But it brought Mr. Hawtrey in something like **a** hundred thousand pounds for all that.

But I am harping on the chances of failure. Let us imagine

that your reception is an enthusiastically cordial one, that the house "rises" to receive you, and breaks into cheer after cheer. Then drink it in and enjoy it, for it will be the sweetest music your ears will ever hear. Make the most of it, and remember it, for you will never hear such strains twice. The same applause and the same cheers may greet you another time, but they will be to you merely an index from which you can judge the price your play will fetch.

You will not get much sleep that night, and the next morning you will be up betimes, and off to the newspaper shop. You will, in all probability, have paid either Messrs. Romeike or Messrs. Curtice a guinea, for which sum they will send you a hundred "notices." If these are flattering, and describe you as "promising," or "coming," you will consider it the cheapest guinea's worth of pleasure you have ever bought. If the papers consider your play a "weak and crude production," and wonder how any manager could have been induced to put on such a farrago of nonsense and ill taste, then you will wish that you had spent your one pound one in having rides on the switchback railway. But, on the whole, the notices are likely to be favourable and encouraging. To the two extremes of authorship, the very old and well established, and the beginners, the critics are very gentle.

You will not have had patience, however, to wait for Messrs. Curtice or Romeike's little boys, and will, as I have said, be off to buy newspapers the first thing in the morning. You will come back, reading one as you walk along, and carrying the rest under your arm, and will wander into the road, and up against carts and cabs, and step on people, and look up, when they swear at you, with a vacant, gaping expression.

This excitement, also, will hardly outlive your first play. After a little while, the only opinion you will care for will be the opinion of the public as expressed at the box-office.

CHAPTER IX.

MONETARY.

AND now for the £ s. d. part **of** the matter—the most important **part** of the matter from the majority of people's point of view. **Your** artist has painted his picture, your poet has sung his song, your cobbler has cobbled his shoes, your preacher has preached his **sermon,** your organ grinder has ground **out** his **tune,** your dramatist has written his play, and the **great** question with one and all is, what shall I get for it**?** What is it going to bring me in ?

They are all **quite right.** In the Golden Age, perhaps, men laboured for love, **as the** foolish birds still sing and the unbusiness-like flowers scent the summer air ; but now, in this hard iron age, we only work for gold ; and the man that asks for less the world despises as **either** fool or hypocrite.

So, unless you wish to encourage roguery (and Heaven knows there's enough in the world without your help) by letting others reap the harvest of your brain, by all means see that you get your fair price for your work. But don't keep the question too much in front of you while you are working. If you work merely for money, you'll find you'll make very little money. It is an undoubted fact that, in the long run, and taking things as a whole, it is the best work that pays best, and the best work—nay, no work at all worthy the name, can be done while your mind is filled with the dreamings of a huckster and the cogitations of a cheapjack. When once your work is finished and in your pocket, and you are going about trying to find a customer for it, then be as sharp, aye, and as grasping, and mercenary, and sordid even, as you can be, or you'll be done. But while you are working you must be an artist, and work for Art's sake. Let the hacks, devoid of brain and heart, roll off the rubbish of a day, and snatch the passing coins the careless crowd flings to them for their tumbling. If you are an artist, you will find it the best policy to do only artistic work.

After which little homily we will come to figures.

There are false impressions abroad concerning dramatic authors and their takings. It is popularly supposed that a successful play brings its author in from one to two hundred thousand pounds, and when I was young and used to believe this stuff, I used to wonder why it was that popular dramatists lived so quietly in little houses at St. John's Wood or Brixton, instead of having two or three palaces each in different parts of the country. When I came to understand matters, however, I found that they did not receive such large incomes as I had imagined. Still, a very comfortable living may be earned by playwriting, and the returns to the author are certainly far in excess of those in any other branch of literature.

There are two methods of dealing with plays—one by sale, the other by "royalties," the latter of which is by far the most generally employed.

Indeed, now that the author's share forms so large a proportion of the profits in a piece, it is hardly possible that any out-and-out sale of all his rights could be arranged. A successful play is a property well worth from £20,000 to £30,000 ; and an author would be foolish to part with all his rights in a piece he had any faith in, for anything under £3,000 to £4,000. On the other hand, the MS. of a play, if a failure, is only worth 1¼d. a lb., so that a speculator would not care to risk so large a sum, especially seeing how impossible it is to say beforehand whether a piece, however good, will take with the public. One thousand pounds would be, I should say, the most that would ever be paid down for a piece ; and a manager would need a deal of faith in an author before he parted even with that sum.

As a rule, the only plays that are bought outright are dramas of the transpontine or provincial school, for which £50 or £100 would be considered a handsome price, and plays written specially to suit some artiste, such as *My Sweetheart* and *Hans the Boatman*, &c., pieces which would be comparatively valueless if left to stand alone. Young authors also often sell their pieces outright, being only too glad to get it accepted anyhow, and rightly arguing to themselves that it is better for them to get it out, and have the advertisement, even if they have to let it go for an old song, as the saying is, than to lose a chance which may not come again for years.

Still, I would advise them not to part with it *too* recklessly. Youth has to pay its footing in all trades. Charles Dickens only got £500 for a book that must have brought in £50,000 ; and Thackeray wrote his best work for the wages of an artizan ; and a young dramatist can't expect, with his first play, to take the footing of a Sims or Pinero. But there is a limit to all things, and there is no necessity to *give away* the labour of months, if not years. A little firmness and tact will often obtain reasonable terms, where an impatient young author is only too eager to give up every advantage. If a man offers to buy your play at all, it means that he wants it, and that there's something in it. A good play is a very rare thing to get hold of, and is worth a price. How to manage in any particular case will, of course, depend upon the circumstances, and you must use your own judgment ; I cannot advise you. All I say is, keep your head cool.

The purchase of particular rights in a play, such as the American rights, the Australian rights, the provincial rights, &c., is a common enough thing ; but this is after the play has been produced and proved successful. The American rights are of great value—almost as valuable as the English rights. There are special firms in America who make it their business to look after the works of English authors out there, and collect and remit them their fees. Nearly all the successful plays, and especially the melodramas produced in London, are played all through the States, and bring in the English authors very handsome returns. Still, if you can get anything like a reasonable sum, I would strongly advise you to sell the American right out and out as soon as possible. They are an enterprising people across the herring pond, and it is not always easy to obtain your fees.

So also with Australia ; £100 at your bankers in London is well worth £200 owing to you in New South Wales.

The provincial rights I hardly see the wisdom of ever parting with. You can never expect to get, in a lump sum down, anything approaching in amount to what "royalties" would, under usual circumstances, bring you in; and, unless you are very hard up for ready money, I should say stick to all British rights, you cannot very easily miss your fees in England, Ireland, or Scotland.

The other system, the "royalty" system of payment, may itself be subdivided into two methods, the one the payment of a stated sum per night, the other the payment of a percentage on the gross takings. The latter system is the one most usually adopted with regard to London, the former as regards the provinces. The payment per night, if a fixed sum, varies from £1 up to £9. One pound a night would be fair enough to pay for a country drama—that is, one written for and produced in the country ; and £9 would be readily given for a "London success "—that is, a piece that **has had a** moderate run and tolerable notoriety at some West-end house.

Adaptations are also commonly paid **for by a** fixed sum—you will come down to adapting very soon. You will start with the high resolve **to** uphold the dignity of **your** profession and **your** country, and scorn the **idea** of being **the mere** purveyor **of** other men's thought. After a few years you will take kindly to Bowdlerising French indecencies, and cooking up German horse play, and terming the result *your* " new and original play." This was done not many years ago by thieving **English** play-wrights without giving the foreign author one **halfpenny. Now,** however, the anxiety **to** get hold of new French and **German** successes has forced **a certain** amount **of** honesty **into the** matter ; for it **is** a law of nature that nothing can work for any length of time **upon a** foundation of dishonesty. Managers and authors keep **a look out** at Paris **and** Berlin, and the moment **a** good play shows its head the English rights are bought from the author, and the piece secured to the purchaser in this country under a system of international copyright, which will be explained in the next chapter. Then some native author is given the thing to " adapt," and he is either paid so much down for his work, or he takes so much royalty per night, **or** the adapter secures the play for himself from the foreign author, and then **deals** with it as his own.

Adapting, **it is fair to** add, is not such **an** easy task **as it** sounds. To any **man** of brains I should say writing an original piece would be simpler.

When a play is paid for by percentage, as is the usual method with all leading original plays, five to ten per cent. on the gross receipts **is** the usual fee, and as a good draw will bring into the box-office an average of £200 per night, and will run for from one to two years, and as a couple of provincial companies will be sent round with the piece at the same time, and bring in the author between them fees almost equal to those received from the London house, and as, in addition to this, there is the American and Colonial rights before referred to, and the piece will very likely be revived and have another long run before it is finally laid by, it may be seen that one play may easily be something like a fortune in itself.

If you can get five per cent. for your early pieces, that is as much as you can expect ; ten per cent. is only paid to established popular writers. I have heard of twelve being asked, but that was for a piece that had already been successfully produced, and then they didn't get it. Two authors, of course, share the five or ten per cent., as the case may be, between them.

All the foregoing applies to three or four-act pieces, but curtain raisers are coming to the front just now, and can, if properly worked among the amateurs, be made a very respectable little property. *Uncle's Will*, I believe, brings in Mr. Theyre Smith a steady income of £50 per annum ; and a friend of mine tells me that a little play of his, written many years ago, has returned him an average of £20 a year ever since. The price paid by theatres for first pieces varies from 30s. to £6 a week, and as such pieces are often revived, and are played constantly round the provinces, they well repay writing. It is from the amateurs, however, that the chief income of a one-act play is derived, there always being a fair demand for such pieces among these ladies and gentlemen.

If your curtain-raiser is successful, when produced, take it to Mr. French, of 89, Strand. He won't say much, being a comfortable-looking old gentleman of few words, but for 3s. a printed page he will publish it, and put it in his list, sending you fifty copies, which you can write pretty dedications in, and send round to all the girls you know. He will also collect your fees from the amateurs, and, after deducting his commission, hand you over the balance each month. As I have said, a good one-act play will be used pretty frequently by the various A.D.

clubs and societies about the country, and, for each performance of it, Mr. French **will** charge them ten or fifteen shillings, or **a** guinea.

Anything beyond a one-act piece, however, it is not safe to **have** published, because, under **the** American copyright laws, **a** play, published over here in book **form,** can be sneaked **and** performed over there for nothing. One-act pieces don't matter. They **are** rarely used **in** America, and the American right of them is, consequently, next to *nil.* Of any big play, likely to be sought after by the amateurs, let Mr. French have two or three neatly-typed copies, **which** he will loan round when required. But, there, **don't listen to me.** Go **to the** shop, **and** business-like Mr. Hogg, the manager, will advise you the best thing **to** do, and **you can't do** better than follow **his advice.**

Well, there **you** are. I've told you what you *can* get for a play, now all you've **got to** do is to go and get it ; and, when you've got it, don't **spend it** recklessly. Seriously, though, if you do get £10,000 for a play that has taken you three months to write, don't go reckoning your income at £40,000 per annum. for the rest of your life, and start living **up** to it. This advice might be given, too, to some authors I know who are not exactly beginners, and who ought to know how few and far between successes are.

At present rates, **two or** three **lucky hits** are sufficient to set a man up for life if **he is** prudent. I wonder if the ghosts of the old dramatists who drudged and starved on the paltry pittance their glorious works brought in to them ever feel a pang of envy shoot through their shadowy breasts, when they look down (or maybe up), and see us, their puny descendants, glutted with the fat of the land. The **work of** Shakespeare's whole life never brought him in what **can be** won now-a-day by adapting a German farce. Fourpence, I see, from an antiquarian magazine, **is** what an author was paid in early days for writing a miracle **play, the** entry running :—

G

" Itm. Pd. Peter ffor writinge the play, 4d." (I wonder if Peter had much difficulty in getting that play accepted.) Buckstone received from first to last £100 for the *Green Bushes*, one of the most successful and constantly-played dramas of the last generation ; and Cary died with a halfpenny in his pocket, while his pieces were filling the theatre night after night.

For the improvement in our position, we dramatists have principally to thank Scribe in France, and W. S. Gilbert in our own country. Before Scribe's time, authors considered themselves happy with a few pounds for a drama, and what induced them to write plays instead of devoting their time to some more profitable employment is a mystery. Scribe, however, by combining his brethren together, and introducing a sort of trades unionism among them, soon changed all that, much to the disgust and indignation of the Parisian managers, and the good work that Scribe commenced in France, Gilbert completed in England by insisting upon the ten per cent. principle.

We have very little to grumble at now.

CHAPTER X.

LEGAL.

THIS will be **a very long, and, I fear, a** dry chapter, but, nevertheless, **I advise you to read it.** If the advantage to you bears any approximation to the labour it has entailed **on me it** will prove of much service to you.

The laws relating to theatrical affairs have been fearfully and wonderfully made, and they grow more confused, contradictory, and unintelligible with every fresh **attempt** to elucidate them. They appeared **to** me somewhat **complicated and** mysterious even before **I went,** for the purposes of these articles, thoroughly into the matter. **Now** that I understand them—as far as human understanding *can* cope with them—the Chinese grammar seems straightforwardness itself compared with them. A vague notion is hovering through my distracted brain that an author can claim no right **in his** work at all, and that anybody can slap his head, and take his play away from him, and that he has no legal redress whatever ; and as one justification among many **for this opinion of mine, I** may mention that at the date I am writing, **a** certain person is advertising in the American papers that he has adapted **Mr.** Rider Haggard's "She" for the stage (without the author's permission, mind), and threatening anyone who does the same (including **Mr.** Rider Haggard himself) with **all** the penalties of **the law**; and really it is a question of **grave** argument if **the law is not on his side.**

A sort of custom of the trade has grown up, regulating all dealings connected with plays, and this, among honest men, answers well enough in practice; but it rests on no sure legal foundation, and, were managers and authors to examine too minutely into the abyss of law over which they exist, they would probably go mad.

The whole confusion arising from its being undecided (and it never will, I expect, be decided) whether there is any "common law" right, as it is termed, in literature. The great wieght of judicial opinion is against there being this right, but some of the judges hold that there is such right, so that uncertain as law is in every case it is just fifty times more uncertain than ever in all theatrical matters.

Now, by "common law"—I am sorry to be a bore, but I must get you to thoroughly understand this preliminary point of the matter, so much depends upon it. By "common law" is meant the law that is established, not by Act of Parliament, but by plain justice and common sense; or to quote a celebrated judge, "by the common law is meant those principles, usages, and rules of action applicable to the government and security of person and property which do not rest for their authority upon any express declaration of the Legislature." If you devote your brains and labour to making a three-legged stool, that stool is yours by right of common law. No one may steal it from you, or injure it, or lay a finger on it without your permission. It is yours from the hour you make it till the crack of doom (unless somebody very heavy sits down on it, and, even then, the pieces belong to you). No one dare dispute your claim to it, and every court in the land will protect you in the enjoyment of that three-legged stool. But if you devote your time to writing a **play or a book, the** law washes its hands of you, and leaves you **to** the mercy of **a** bunch of ill-worded, involved, and **not-to-be** understood statutes, **under which you** can **be robbed and** swindled with impunity by every dirty blackguard **who may be** hanging **on to** the fringe of the theatrical profession.

" Yes," says the judge, adjusting his spectacles, " A. **wrote** the play, and B. stole it from him. That, I take it, **is clear.** Now, I will carefully consider the Act, and **then give** my judgment accordingly."

In nine cases out **of ten the judgment is for B., and A. has to** pay the costs.

In " Murray *v.* Elliston " (to go no further back) Byron's tragedy of *Marino Faliero*, the copyright of which belonged to **Mr.** Murray, had been taken and altered, and performed as a play at Drury **Lane. If ever** there was **a** case of cool and impudent robbery it was here. **Verdict** for **the** defendant.

Another famous case, in which the principle of there being no common law-right in literary work **was** maintained, is " Reade *v.* Conquest." Mr. Reade argued, among other points, that the performance of Mr. Conquest's play—adapted from his (Mr. Reade's) novel, " It's Never **Too** Late To Mend "— injured the sale of the book, **and** also prevented him himself from making the use of the tale as a play, thereby claiming, as the judge pointed out, a common law right in his work ; and, although Reade won the case, as we shall see hereafter, when dealing more fully with the case under another branch of the subject, **he** failed entirely on this head, the Court holding that an author had no common **law** right **in** his play, " that the time had passed when the question was open to discussion, and that it must **now** be considered to be settled that copyright in a published work only exists by statute."

In " Turner *v.* Robinson " the Master of Rolls (Ireland) said, " Works of literature are unprotected by the common law."

In " Toole *v.* Young," **Lord** Chief Justice Cockburn said, " The author of a drama is not protected by the common law."

On the **other hand,** Judge Erle, in " Jeffreys *v.* Boosey," held most strongly that there *was* a **common law** right in coypright and stageright (" Stageright," **a word** invented by the late Chas. Reade, and now **generally** adopted, implies the right of a **dramatist in his plays similar to the " copyright "** enjoyed by an **author in his books); and** the following sentences from his judgment are worth recording :—

" The right of an author in his works is analogous to the rights of ownership in other **personal** property.

"In other matters the (common) **law has been adapted to** the progress **of society according to justice** and convenience, and by analogy it **should be the same** for **literary** works, and **they should become property with all** its incidents on the most **elementary principles of securing to** industry its fruits and to capital its profits."

And he, **Judge Erle, concluded his** exhaustive and closely **argued decision with these** words :—" **Upon this** review of **principle and authority, I submit that authors have** property in **their works by common law as** well since the statute of Anne **as before it."** (It had been argued that even if such right had **previously existed, the Copyright Act, passed in** the reign of Queen Anne, had destroyed it.)

Lord St. Leonards, in the same case, it should be mentioned, however, held just the opposite opinion to Erle.

Another eloquent judge, **Judge Aston, may also be** quoted on the same side :—" The invasion of this sort of property (literary property) is as much **against** every man's sense of it as it is against natural reason and moral rectitude. It is against the conviction of every man's own breast who attempts it. He knows it not to be his own. He knows he injures another, and he does not do it for the sake of the public, but treacherously and for mere gain (*animo lucrnadi*).". " The law of nature and truth and the light of reason and the common **sense of** mankind is against it."

And, to conclude our quotations, Judge Dodderidge, speaking of the same subject, asks, " Why should the **common law be** deemed so narrow and illiberal as not to recognise and **receive** under **its** protection a **property** so circumstanced **as the** present ? "

So much for general **introduction** ; now let **us** examine **into** details.

The rights—such as they are—of a **dramatic author in the** play he has written are given to him by **special statutes which** have been passed from **time to** time, beginning **with the famous** Copyright Act, **" 8 Anne, c. 19 "** ; and into these rights I propose to wade.

To **state** them **with** any certainty **is** impossible. A council **of the best** lawyers **in** the kingdom could **not** do that. The **exact** meaning of a statute is always **a** matter of argument, **much** to the advantage of the arguers. **One** judge thinks it means one thing and another judge holds that the words must **be taken** to imply the opposite ; **and if you do ever have** to go **to** law over any of your plays, I pity you.

Now, first of all, let us understand what it is we are going **to** talk about. This is **always** a great point gained in every **argu-** ment. The Act declares **the** matter to which it refers **to be** "any tragedy, **comedy,** play, opera, farce, and any **other** dramatic piece or entertainment "; and how **wide** an **area** the Courts allow the definition to cover may **be** judged by the fact **that in** " Russell *v.* Smith," a mere song, entitled "The Ship on Fire," sung by a gentleman in evening dress, and without any scenic accessory, was deemed **a "** dramatic piece " within the meaning of the Act, it being of a descriptive character, and the supposed words of the persons on board being employed. Any of Sims's ballads would, by the same reasoning, be held to be dramatic pieces, and Mr. Sims could, if he chose, control their recitation.   Indeed, half of the recitations one hears at smoking concerts, &c., could, I should argue from this decision, be deemed dramatic pieces, and their performance protected.

Such being your property, what are your rights in it?

Before publication, your work belongs to you by right of common law, that is, so long as your play remains unacted it is your property in the same way that your hat and boots are your property, and anyone interfering with it can be dealt with simply and expeditiously by the common law.

This may not, at first sight, appear much of a privilege, but there might arise circumstances under which the principle would confer distinct advantage on the author.   For instance, if you lent your play to some man to read before it was " published " (the " publication " of a play is its first public performance), and he took it, or a copy of it, and performed it without your permission, that would be a simple robbery, and could be stopped at once.   Were matters otherwise your only remedy would be an expensive and uncertain law-suit.

Nor could anyone " crib " any scenes or ideas from it—the proof that he had done so, however, would rest with you, and as, if he did do such a thing, he would be pretty sure to alter and disguise them, and would then argue that they were his own, you would have extreme difficulty in establishing the fact.

You can allow your unpublished play to be performed privately (the distinction between a private and a public performance I will describe later on) without in the least perilling your rights.

Printing a play in book form, and selling it over a counter, is not deemed a " publication " of the play, and does not injure your stage-right *in Her Majesty's dominions.*   But it deprives you of your chances in America at once.   A play, as I have said, is not considered published until it has been publicly performed. To take an example, you can write a play and have it published in a book or magazine without endangering your stage-right in it as a play. **Some** time ago a comedietta was published in *The Lady's Pictorial.* All the acting rights of that comedietta remain with the author, and nobody can touch it any way.*

Selling the book copyright in a play does not carry with **it** the sale of the stageright.

Mr. W. S. Gilbert's plays are published in **book form, and** sold all over England. Now I **do not know whether Mr. Gil-**bert has sold the book copyright of **those plays to the publisher,** or whether he **and** the publisher share **profits, or what the**

---

* Some friends have taken objection to my view of the law on **this** point and doubt the safety of first publishing a play in book form. It would, of course, be absurd to dogmatise upon such a very shifty science as Law ; and, as a question of expediency, I should **advise** any author *not* to publish his play as a book before having it performed ; but, nevertheless, I feel tolerably sure of my ground ; and I believe that any manager performing without the consent of the author, any play first published in book form would get the worst of the argument. The Act (5 and 6 Victoria—clause 22) distinctly states that the sale of the book copyright of a play does not carry with it the right of representation. If the law expressly withholds the *stageright* from the purchaser of the *copyright* of a play, it surely would not throw open such stage-right to every outsider. Again, the law actually directs a foreign author, wishing to secure his play in this country, to **first** publish a translation of such a play in book form, and *Frou-Frou* **was first published** here in the columns of a magazine.

Nor have practical experiments of the kind been wanting. Not very long ago " Ouida " published a thoroughly actable little play, reserving **at** the same time the stageright. Surely a play with the name of " Ouida " attached to it would have been worth stealing, and there is no lack of thieves hanging round the theatrical profession. **Some** years **back** a series of one-act plays appeared in **a** now defunct paper—*The Play.* Many of these were quite actable, and one of them, written by the late Palgrave Simpson, would have been well worth putting on at any theatre. It has not been touched. There are plays on Mr. French's list which have never been publicly performed, and fairly good little comediettas often appear in the various magazines. The explanation is that while the author of a narrative possesses only one right in his work, namely, that of copyright, his more fortunate brother, the author of a drama, possesses both copyright *and* stageright, and can dispose of the **two** rights separately. Lastly, a play, until it been publicly performed, belongs to the author by right of *Common Law.*

arrangement is ; but, for the sake of argument, we will suppose that he has sold the copyright out-and-out to the publisher. This does not give the publisher any right to *act* the plays, or to deal with them upon the stage in any way. The exact words of the statute are " no assignment of the copyright of any book consisting of, or containing a dramatic piece shall be holden to convey to the assignee the right of representing or performing such dramatic piece." " Book " here includes any article story, &c., &c., published in any magazine or newspaper.

But such publication in book form *does* deprive you of the American right, so don't print any play you think you can do anything with over there. Every play printed and sold for 6d. over Messrs. French's counter can, under the American law, be played anywhere in the United States without the English author being paid a halfpenny.

Of course, mere printing for private circulation, without publishing, is only like having so many copies of the play written or typed out, and carries with it no legal effect. Indeed, at most of the theatres now, new plays are always printed for rehearsal and other purposes instead of beings copied out in writing as formerly.

So much for your rights before publication. Now, assuming your piece to have been published, *i.e.*, performed in public, let us examine into what rights you then possess over it.

CHAPTER XI.

LEGAL (*continued*).

IN not very ancient days, dramatic authors had little, if any, rights at law over the representation of their works ; and the only practical means they could adopt for protection was that of being careful that there was only one copy of their play, and that that copy did not get into the hands of unscrupulous persons, who would keep it, or make a copy of it, and so be able to perform the play without their consent. They must have had an anxious time.

In William IV.'s reign, however, a bill was obtained, principally through the exertions of Sir Bulwer Lytton, conferring upon dramatists a distinct control over the performance of their pieces, and subsequent legislation has steadily improved our position.

By Bulwer Lytton's Act—the first Act in which "stage right," as distinct from " copyright, the right of multiplying printed copies of a book," was recognised as a property—the author of a dramatic piece (the definition of which we settled in our last chapter) was given the " sole liberty of representing it, or causing it to be represented, at any place of dramatic entertainment in any part of the British dominions."

By " place of dramatic entertainment," it has been decided, by the Courts and the Act between them, to mean any place to which admission is charged for *either directly or indirectly*, or any place in which wine, beer, or spirits ("excisable liquor") shall be sold. A performance in such a place consitutes a public performance. In this way, Lady Campbell's garden, when *As You Like It* was played there, and a guinea charged for admission, would have been a "place of dramatic entertainment."

The payment for admission need not be by money taken at the doors, nor even by previous purchase of tickets. "The purchase of any article being made a condition for any person to see a stage play," is held by the Act to be proof that the performance is taking place "for hire," and no piece must be played "for hire" except in a place licensed for "dramatic entertainment." Some amateur dramatic clubs refuse to pay author's fees on the ground that the performances are private, that no money is taken at the doors, and no tickets sold.. But I very much doubt, having regard to the words of the Act I have just quoted, whether their contention would hold good; and it would certainly be worth while for authors to club together and try a case. It could be argued that, although no money is taken actually on the night of the performance, still the membership to the club, which gives the right of admission, is always charged for, and that thus payment is "indirectly" taken, the purchase of membership in the club being made a condition for such right of entry. That the shirking of the unfortunate author's fees is a mean piece of artful dodgery goes without saying, and, if the few clubs (exceptions to an honourable rule) who practice it, could be compelled to act honestly, it would be better for themselves and society in general.

Lord Coleridge, it may be noticed, in "Shelley *v.* Bethell," declined to adopt, as exclusive test of the privacy of a performance, that "no charge was made for admission."

The definition of a "private" performance received its latest elucidation in "Duck *v.* Bates." The three judges, in that case, held that to constitute a performance a private one it was not sufficient merely that no money was taken, but the performance must be of a "domestic" character, and take place in a *private* building—not a building *hired* for the purpose.

Neither, at a private performance should any programmes be sold, or **any** collection be made.

The consent of the author of any piece to its performance or performances must, in strictness, be "first had and obtained in writing." But, of course, in practice the consent is, under ordinary circumstances, assumed.

Now, before we go any further, it may be as well to inquire here, into who is the **"author" of** a piece, **and who is the** proprietor and owner of the stageright therein.

As a general rule, **as** in the case of a man sitting down and writing a play "all out of his own head." The author is by law the proprietor. But, sometimes a writer is employed by a manager or other person to write for him, and then the case is **not** so simple.

First of all, it has been decided, in "Shepherd *v.* Conquest," that a man cannot be hired at so much wages to write a play. Literature is, very properly, not permitted by our Courts to be dealt with on the same footing as tinkering or tailoring. You can engage a carpenter at two pounds a week to make a table for you, and when that table is made, it belongs to you. But if you engage a dramatist as your servant, and set him to work to write a play, that play, when done, is not yours but his. **In** "Shepherd *v.* Conquest" the proprietors of the Surrey Theatre employed a Mr. Courtney to go to Paris for them and adapt a certain French piece then being played there, they paying him travelling expenses, and **a** weekly salary. This was done, the adaptation being called *Old Joe and Young Joe*, and the Surrey Managers took possession of it, under the belief that Mr. Courtney having been, as it were, their paid workman in the matter the result of his work belonged to them. Courtney, who, **to say** the least of it, seems to have been pretty sharp, however, in spite of this, dealt with the piece as his own, and the court upheld him in doing so. Chief Justice Jervis in his judgment, said : " that the intention of the legislature in the enactments relating to copyright was to elevate and **protect** literary men ; that such an intention **could** only be effectuated by holding that the actual composer of the work **was the** author and proprietor of the copyright, and that no relation existing between him and an employer who himself took **no intellectual part in the** production **of the work** could, without an assignment in writing, vest the proprietorship of it in the latter " ; **and** he decided that as no such assignment in writing had been made the piece still belonged to **Courtney.**

But where the manager or other person who is bringing **out** the play arranges **and** plans the production himself, and employs one or more authors **to write special parts—mere** accessories to the whole scheme—then the portions so written by those authors belong not to them, but **to the** manager—the organiser of the whole scheme.

In this way, presuming, as I **believe was the** case, that Mr. Irving employed Mr. Frank Marshall to make for a specified sum the alterations and additions required in *Werner*, those alterations and additions belong not to their author, Mr. Marshall, but to their author's employer and the organiser of the whole production, Mr. Irving, and this without **any assignment from Mr. Marshall.**

This principle was **fixed in "Hatton *v.* Kean."** Mr. Kean **had "organised" a play, and had** employed Mr. **Hatton to** compose a piece of **music** as part of **the** performance. **Held :** "that the music so **composed** by the direction and under the superintendence of the defendant, and **as part** of the general plan of the spectacle," was the property **of the defendant. In** all subsequent cases of the kind the same ruling **has held good.**

In **a** similar **way, an author can** engage other **writers to** assist him in his **work.** He might engage one man to write songs to be sung by one or more of the characters, and another man to write him a curse for the villain to pronounce, and a third man to write him a love scene, and yet the **whole play** would belong to him, just as a picture, that his pupils have helped him to paint, belongs to an artist.

All that is necessary is that the portions and matter so composed by the employés shall **be** accessory to the whole, and shall be a " part and parcel " of it, and not independent pieces, and that they shall be composed *under the direction, and with the intellectual assistance* of the employer.

Sir J. Leach, with **reference** to this subject, said, in " Barfield *v.* Nicholson," " **I am of opinion that under the** statute the person who forms the plan, and who embarks in the speculation of a work, and **who** employs various persons to compose different parts of it, adapted to their own peculiar acquirements —that he, the person who so forms the plan and scheme of the work, and pays different artists of his own selection, who upon certain conditions contribute to it, is the author and proprietor of the work."

The mere suggestion of the subject by another person, and even his alterations and improvements (?) do not give him any title to any share in the authorship. Even his giving you the whole plot would not entitle him **to** any such share, except with your consent. Joint authorship **or "**collaboration," as **it is** termed, must be the result of preconcerted joint design.

And now with regard to the vexed and complicated question of " adapting " plays from novels and tales.

Up **to** within a few months ago—that is up to the Spring of 1888, anyone could legally "adapt," or, in plain language, steal, another man's novel or tale, and make a play of it without his consent and without paying him one halfpenny, or acknowledging him in any way.

By the disgraceful condition of our copyright laws no " stage-right " in his work is reserved to the author of any novel—and by the word " novel " please remember I mean to include any tale, or story, or poem, published either by itself or in any magazine, or newspaper, or journal. He can prevent its being printed and sold without his permission, but he cannot prevent its being **acted.**

In " Reade *v.* **Conquest,"** Mr. Reade wrote a novel called " It's Never Too Late to Mend." Another man adapted it for the stage without Reade's consent, **and** such adaptation was played at the Grecian Theatre. Held **" that** representing the incidents **of a** published novel in **a** dramatic form upon the stage, although done publicly and for profit, is no infringement of copyright." **Mr.** Reade won this particular case in the end, but it was upon an entirely distinct argument.

In " Toole *v.* Young " the **same** ruling was maintained. **Mr.** Hollingshead (" one Hollingshead " as the reports **have** it, as if there were room in this world **for two** John Hollingsheads), **wrote a** novel and published it **in** *Good Words.* H. P. Grattan " adapted " that novel for the stage, and the piece was performed **under** the title of *Glory.* **Held " that however** shabby and discreditable it may seem " (**I** am quoting the Judge's words) " any **person has a** right to dramatise the novel without being liable **to an** action on the ground that Mr. Hollingshead **had the** copyright."

Other **cases** could **be cited, but they would** merely go to prove **the same fact, viz., that the** work of a man's brain, if put into **" book** " form, could **be sneaked** from him, and acted **on the stage, not only without the** interference of, but with the **actual protection of the Law !**

The only safeguard that the author of a novel **had** against us " dramatists " was the expensive, cumbersome, **and,** for many of them, quite impossible plan of dramatising their story themselves, and getting it publicly **performed before** they published it as **a** book.

But we **have** changed all that. The Law remains the same

as opposed to honesty and justice as it was before. Theoretically **you** can still appropriate stories and "adapt" novels to the stage, **but** practically, except in the very unlikely event of the famous **decision in** Warne *v.* Seebohm being reversed, the theatrical **Dick** Turpin's long **career is over.**

By a legal quibble, as brilliant as that raised for the defendant in Shylock *v.* Antonio, a long-standing evil has been swept away. Trickery has been called upon to take up the lance **for** Justice against Law ; and to **the** delight **of** all **decent men,** Law has been defeated. *The Little Lord Fauntleroy* case **is too** familiar just at present **to** need recalling ; but, **to** make this **chapter** complete, I will briefly state it.

Mrs. Burnett wrote a book called " Little Lord Fauntleroy," and assigned the English copyright to Messrs. Warne. A **Mr.** Seebohm " adapted " **the story** to **the** stage, as thousands of adapters before him had adapted thousands **of** novels ; and the piece **was** played at the Prince of Wales's Theatre. Mrs. Burnett, through Messrs. Warne, objected, as thousands of adapted novelists had before objected ; and went to law, as tens **of** objecting novelists had done before, to enforce her objections ; and everybody laughed at her, and said she was only throwing her money away, and that she was bound to lose the day, as all her predecessors **had.**

But Mrs. **Burnett's legal** advisers were geniuses, and they won the day for her ; **and, now** that they **have shown** how easy and simple it is for **a** novelist to protect his **property, there is** little fear of thieves breaking through and stealing in future. The Copyright Act, as I have already pointed out, does not protect an author against having his story acted on the stage ; but **it** does most emphatically assert that no one shall multiply copies of his book, *or of any part of his book.* " Very well," said Mrs. Burnett's counsel to Mr. Seebohm, "play Little Lord Fauntleroy as much as you like. We cannot prevent that. But you have sent a copy of the play you have made out of the novel to the

H

Lord Chamberlain. In that copy of the play there are passages taken from the novel. You have thus multiplied copies of parts of the novel. The Copyright Act forbids you to do this, and the copy of your play in which such copy parts occur is forfeit to our clients; and we demand of the Lord Chamberlain that he give it up. This plea was successfully upheld by the Court, and the copy of the play lodged for licensing purposes at the Lord Chamberlain's office was given up to Messrs. Warne; and as the Lord Chamberlain cannot or will not license a play unless a copy of it is in his possession, and as no play can be performed without his license, the piece had to be withdrawn.

It has been suggested in some quarters that Seebohm might have evaded the law by cutting out the portions of the book he desired to use, and pasting them on the pages of his play; it being argued that this would not be multiplying copies, but only using up copies bought from the rightful owners. But the idea will not bear consideration by anyone acquainted with law. Whether the copy was faked up with scissors and paste, or written out it would be just the same—the work of the would-be pirate; and the copy would be issued by him, not by the owner of the copyright, the only person entitled to issue copies.

Of course, all this cannot prevent ideas and suggestions being taken from novels; nor is it desirable that it should do so.

CHAPTER XII.

LEGAL *(concluded)*.

LICENSING I have spoken about in a previous chapter. Every play **must** be licensed before performance, and all additions and alterations to old plays must also be licensed. Of course, this is practically needed only in the case of important alterations.

Registering **is** a very particular matter, and should be paid great attention to. At Stationers' Hall, just off Ludgate-hill, a book is kept for the registration **of** "the proprietorship" in the copyright **of** books and plays, and the assignment of such copyright ("copyright" here includes "stageright.") The proprietor of the copyright—that is, the author **of** the play or his assignee—can, **at any** time after the first performance of the play, enter his right **in** this book of registry, and such entry is *prima facie* proof of his proprietorship, but subject to be rebutted by evidence.

The mode of entry **is by** stating the title of the play, the **name** and address of the author (yourself), the name and address of the proprietor (also yourself), unless you have sold the piece, **in** which case leave **it** to the purchaser to **do** all this, and the date and place of its first performance. For making this entry you must pay 5s.

After having registered your proprietorship, you can, for another 5s., make another entry assigning your right to anybody you like—to your wife, for instance, if you are afraid of bankruptcy, or it is otherwise advisable that you should get rid of · your ownership in the piece.

This assignment by mere entry is quite as legal and binding as though it had been done by formal deed, and it saves the stamp.

Indeed, "registration" is the one point where the law is really kind to authors. A simple entry in this registry book, a certified copy of which can be had for five shillings, is, as I have said, legal *prima facie* evidence of ownership, whether as author or assignee, and it rests upon the other side to prove that the entry is wrong.

A wrongful entry will be ordered to be expunged from the book upon application to the Court by the rightful proprietor, and the person who has made the wrongful entry will be punished.

You are not compelled to make this registration at all, and your not doing so will not damage your rights in any way. But you cannot sue until such registration has been made, so that the first thing your solicitor will do, upon being instructed by you to proceed against anyone for infringing your play, is to go to Stationers' Hall and see that you are duly registered as proprietor of the play. If it has not been done already he will do it then, and that will be quite sufficient.

Titles are regarded as trade marks ; you must not use another man's title, nor a "colourable imitation," of it, for the same class of work. The principle upon which the Court will act in the matter is that of preventing the public from being deceived as to what work is really being offered to them. You would not be allowed just now to write a three-act comic opera, and call

it *Dorothy*, because that would be a palpable attempt **to trade**
upon the popularity of the Prince of Wales's piece. **But** you
would be allowed (probably, not certainly) **to** call a melodrama
or a one-act farce *Dorothy*, because there could be no pretence
then **that you** were trying to make the public believe that **your**
play **was Mr.** Cellier's.

It would just depend **upon the view the** judge took **of the**
matter ; **and** it would **save trouble and bother if you** adopted
some other title altogether.

I hope it will **be** needless for me **to caution you** against
writing anything immoral, or of a nature **calculated to** bring
public institutions into contempt (please don't **do this), or** anything to injure or caricature public or private individuals. If
you write anything **of** this kind the Lord Chamberlain will
refuse **to** license it ; **or if it does** by chance slip through his
fingers at the time of reading, it will be prohibited afterwards
(as **the** author of *The Happy Land*, in which Messrs. Righton,
Fisher and Hill brought Mr. Gladstone and Messrs. Lowe and
Ayrton into contempt, could tell **you**).

The term for which your **play is** protected **is** during your
lifetime and for seven years afterwards, or for forty-two years
from the date of its first performance, whichever period may be
the longer. **After** this, **it is** public property.

"Stageright" in a play **is** a legal property, and can be assigned,
or bequeathed, or, in fact, dealt with just as **any** other form of
property may be.

As regards international stageright, the question is a big one,
but I propose **to** go into it only so far as English authors are
affected.

At the end of 1887 **a** new copyright convention came into
operation as between England and certain foreign countries.
It has not really altered matters very much in effect from what
they were before ; but it has done away with a good deal of

harassing detail formerly necessary to be gone through, especially **by** foreign authors desiring to secure copyright with us.

The countries included in the convention are France, Germany, Belgium, Italy, Spain, Haïti, Liberia (wherever that may be), Tunis, and Switzerland. In those nine countries the English author **can secure a** limited stageright for his play, provided he publishes a translation of **his play** in such country or countries within ten years after **its original** production. If he allow the ten years **to** go by without doing this, his play is public property in those countries. The course of proceeding in each case will depend **upon the laws** and customs **of the** particular country, and can be carried out effectively **only** through some foreign agent. Practically speaking, this part of the matter is unimportant. English plays are rarely required **abroad.** The **boot is** on the other foot.

Plays brought out **in any of these countries** can likewise be protected **in** England, and, as this **affects the** greater industry of adaptation, we must examine into the matter.

The foreign author sells his British right to **an Englishman** It need not be to **an** Englishman. **It** need **not be to anyone** He, the foreign author, may **carry the matter through himself.** But I am, **for** the sake of example, taking the ordinary custom. The course **that** the English purchaser had then **to** follow used **to** be a most expensive and dangerous one, **full of** complicated formalities, the slightest bungling over any one of which **would** ruin the whole work. (The rights in *Frou Frou* were lost **merely** because **Mr.** Edwards' **translation was not, in parts, a** sufficiently literal **one**).

Literal translations had to be **made and published within** given periods, copies lodged at **the public libraries, the work** registered at Stationers' Hall, &c., **&c., &c. All** this **is now** needless, and it is only required that a translation or adaptation of the original foreign play be published **in book form or** produced at a theatre within ten years from the date of its original production abroad. If the ten years go by, and the piece is neither published nor produced then anyone is at liberty to use it.

It is not necessary now (as formerly it was) that the foreign work should be registered in England before translation or adaptation. It is sufficient **for the play to have** been registered in the country of its origin, according **to the laws and** customs of that country.

The purchaser's right to the foreign work only **lasts for ten** years, but, when it is once " adapted," the **adaptation becomes** a play of itself, subject to all the **regulations and rights of an** original work, and belongs to **the adapter or his assignee for the** usual term of **seven** years **beyond the adapter's** lifetime, **or 42** years from the first performance, **whichever** period may be **the** longer.

The Act **finally** proceeds **to completely** stultify itself by expressly stating that it only prohibits adaptations " with non-essential alterations, additions, or abridgments so made as not to confer the character of a new original **work"**; and **it** would thus appear to give the honest purchaser **very** little for his money, as what is the use of his purchasing the rights from the foreign author, and going **to** all **the** trouble **and** expense of registering, translating, &c., when, by making his adaptation a little freer than usual, and hacking it about sufficiently to enable him to argue that he had made " essential alterations, &c.," he could take it for nothing. But, **if the Act** is framed foolishly, the courts have decided to administer **it** wisely. In " Wood *v* Chart " **the** judge stated very clearly that **if** the first and authorised adaptation had been in order, **and** he had been asked to prohibit **the** second and unauthorised adaptation on **the** ground of its being a " piratical translation," he would have done so ; and there is no doubt that the legitimate proprietor of any adaptation would be upheld by the courts in preventing the performance of, to quote the judge's words, " anything like it—anything approaching it."

With respect to all other foreign countries except the nine named we can steal from them and they can steal from us with impunity.

Our copyright and stageright relationships with America are complicated and mysterious. I do not intend to examine into them, as that would be of no practical use. I shall content myself with merely stating the bare facts, as they at present exist, without troubling you with the reasons and explanations.

How the question stands generally, may be judged by the following extract from "Morgan's Law of Literature" (an American authority) : — "It appears, first, that an alien dramatic author in the United States practically and in effect receives precisely the same protection in his literary property as the citizen can receive in his ; and, secondly, that by neglecting to comply with our copyright laws the alien dramatic author can actually enjoy greater privileges of protection in his literary property than he could by complying with them."

So long as you do not publish your play in book form, and sell copies, it cannot be played in America without your consent. One method of dealing with it over there is for you to sell your American rights to a citizen of the United States. Such sale is generally a mere formal matter, the purchaser being your agent, or the agent of the English purchaser out there, and the purchase money being merely nominal—one dollar or so. The piece is then played, and your fees collected and remitted to you by the agent. Of course, if you sell the piece for a sum down to some American manager that simplifies the case. The usual custom, however, is merely for an American manager to take the piece, and remit you the agreed royalties in just the same way as an English manager would.

The American author is not so fortunate as his English brother. Any play produced first in America can be stolen and played in England, as poor Dion Boucicault has learned to his cost. To protect themselves from this robbery American authors now produce their plays through some hole-and-corner performance in England before producing them in America, **as** *Young Mrs. Winthrop* was produced at the Marylebone **Theatre a** few days before it was first played in America, **and the** English stageright thus secured to Mr. Bronson **Howard.**

This method **of** acquiring **the** English **stageright is in accordance** with the provisions **of our Dramatic Copyright Act,** which gives **to a** foreign **author the full British right for his** play, *provided it be first produced in* **this country.**

I think I have now **explained to you pretty fully your legal** rights, privileges, **and** protections **as a dramatist. How to** enforce and maintain those **rights, privileges, and protections** in a court of law—the steps necessary **to recover** your fees, **to** prevent unauthorised performance of **your** plays, to defeat infringement, to guard against piracy or theft—this I do not propose to tell you. It would necessitate a chapter much longer **than** the **present** one, and **be** of no practical use. You could **not conduct** the case yourself. You must put yourself in **the hands of** some solicitor who has made a special study of copyright cases (there are not too many lawyers **who** do thoroughly understand this work. You will **do** well **to** make **a** careful selection). He will know what to **do,** and will **do it,** and your knowing all about it, too (even if **your** unlegally trained mind could understand the **process, which is** doubtful) would be mere surplusage.

All that it **is needful** for you to grasp **with** reference **to** the matter is (1) That if any person shall play any dramatic piece, **or** any part of it, without the consent in writing of the proprietor (or his agent), at any place of dramatic entertainment in **Her** Majesty's dominions, that person shall be liable to payment of various penalties **and** damages. (2) That every action for any offence or injury must be brought within twelve **months** after the offence is committed.

CHAPTER XIII.

CONCLUSION.

AND now, old reader—I say "old reader," just as, if I were talking to you, I should say "old man," because I know you are a man, and a young one to boot. No women, speaking generally, are dramatists, or seem to desire to become so. Seeing how they dominate all other branches of imaginative literature, this is curious. I suppose it is that they are un-dramatic by nature. Their whole mental organisation is opposed to the *directness*, the *silence* which constitute, as it were, the two thunder-clouds from which the lightning of "action" (that is, "drama") springs. Take George Eliot, who, of all women writers, approaches the nearest in her instincts to the dramatic. Two splendid scenes of hers occur to me at this moment, both pregnant with drama in its highest form, and both spoilt, from a dramatic point of view, by eloquent description and philosophical comment. The one is Silas Marner's finding of the child; and the other the death of Maggie Tulliver and her brother, Tom, swamped in the flood, by the old mill, where as children they had lived and played. Scenes such as these, in the hands of a true dramatist, would be made to speak for themselves, and say all that could be said, without one word from the author. Every line of argument or explanation weakens incident. It is like draping a statue. But a woman's mind, I am sure, could never be made to grasp this fact. A woman would never be content to **let** the **audience** *imagine* her **hero's** grief **and** despair. **When** Reginald returns to his home **to find a** note from Anastasia, announcing her departure with Alphonse, the foreign villain, it would **never** be sufficient, in her idea, for Reginald to exclaim, " My God ! " and sink into chair, L. C. " as Curtain, &c." **She** would give Reginald a ten minutes' soliloquy, **in which he** would explain to **the house** by the aid of heartrending adjectives that he was awfully upset—that **he** should never have believed it—that he could'nt understand it—**and** that he had loved her **with a love, &c.** But enough on this subject of women (women are always leading us men astray), and **the** impossibility of their becoming dramatists. **It** is of, and **to,** the people who can and may become dramatists that I wish to say a few parting words. I think I have already **given** all the practical advice and information that it is in my power to give, and these few last words will, therefore, be as few last words generally are, mere exhortation. I shall rather like giving them. Preaching to other people what they should do always was my strong point. I feel then that I am doing good, **and** that without any undue exertion or annoyance to myself. **I** suppose everybody feels the same, and that is why good advice and moral maxims **are** so plentiful in this world ; and that there is always an average of ten or twelve enthusiastic teachers to every one conscientious disciple.

This is an age in which we are all "on the make," and an author's reputation rests not on what he does, but on how much he gets. L.S.D. is the standard of art in this nineteenth century. The manager comes before the curtain, and announces that the nightly receipts have maintained an average of over three hundred pounds, and that the advance booking still continues unabated, and the pit rises up and **cheers**, and the stalls flutter with suppressed delight, and **all** feel that they **are in the** presence of a **great** and good man. **On** the first night, **the** play **appears to a mere plain** intelligence, a **poor, weak,** trashy **thing, badly** constructed, badly written, **with puerile plot,** impossible **characters, and** hackneyed **incidents.** But it runs for a thousand nights and brings in fifty **thousand pounds or so, which proves to** every practical **mind that the** first impressions of the piece were **wrong,** and **that** instead **of being the maudlin balderdash that** a less enlightened age **might have fancied it to be, it is in reality a grand and noble piece of literature. Then we gush over William Snooks, the author, as if he were Homer, and Hugo, and Goethe, and Schiller, and Dickens, and Molière rolled into one.** Did **Shakespeare, or** Ben Jonson, **or Marlowe,** or **Sheridan ever write a play that brought in fifty thousand** pounds ? **No ! Very well then, do not let us hear any** more **about these over-rated old mummies while we've got a** literary **god like Snooks, hanging about.** Managers, actors, brother **authors, critics, and the public generally will respect** you far more **for writing a play by which you gain a fortune, than for** penning the grandest comedy that ever **graced the English stage if it** fails **to "draw."** Against this tendency of the age very **few of us have the strength and courage to do battle. We start full of chivalrous and heroic resolutions. We** respect **ourselves, and we honour our profession. We lay to heart pretty little catch phrases about** the stage **being a** greater **power for good than the pulpit, about** literature being the prophet **of the modern day wilderness ; and** we determine that **our pen shall be drawn only in the service of** honour **and** manhood, and shall dart its **ridicule against only** the mean and **the false ; but, after a time, we seem to find that the service of honour and manhood is a somewhat hard and poorly paid service, and that in the ranks of folly the wage is high and the** promotion rapid, so we quickly right about face and cross over to the enemy.

Still it is advisable, even from the most sordid point of view, not to be too eager for the change, especially if you are at all capable of good work, It is an undoubted fact that in the long run, and taking a man's career as a whole, it is the best writing that pays. Quick, shallow trumpery, trimmed so as to just catch the popular breeze of the moment, may skim along bravely enough during a transient sunny hour, but it is in the great, slow-moving, stately ships, built with long labour, launched with trouble and care, that the solid merchandise of the world is brought home. You want to be a successful dramatic author, not the author of a successful drama. A lucky fluke will make you the latter, but the former can be achieved only by a steady course of sound work. The former is over and done with, and the fortune spent on the " easy come, easy go " principle in a year or two, and you are never heard of again. The latter is a career!

And from other motives—not sordid ones, if you can have patience to listen to such—it is well to aim at only true, honest work. The popularity gained may not be any wider, but it will be far deeper, and, though self-respect is a somewhat costly luxury to indulge in, it is nevertheless a healthy and invigorating one. If you can afford it, that is, if you have a sufficiently manly mind to be content with comfort (which can be purchased anywhere for three hundred a year), and not be craving like a child, for everything you see, then by all means purchase it.

Give the public the deepest and highest you have in you. Do not be afraid that it will be too good for them. Never be satisfied with anything because it's "good enough." Feel that whatever you write is the best that you can do. Then, whether it succeeds or not, it is none of your fault.

Remember that, as a rule, the most lasting work takes the

longest time to do. There may come moments of inspiration
in which you can dash off a certain amount of good stuff quickly.
Such moments are like the two or three hundred yards of level
and half way up the hill over which every now and then the team
will rattle your coach at a spanking gallop, but it is the steady
jog-trot you must depend upon for the day's journey. Do not,
therefore, pride yourself on having " knocked off " an act in one
day. In all probability it will be a day wasted. A couple of
months spent over it will be far better. Writers like Dickens,
Thackeray, Macaulay, and George Eliot took weeks to write a
chapter or two. It is your little twopenny-halfpenny authors—
the sort that would be dear at six for a shilling—that "knock
off" things in a few hours.

Be honest—never mind if you are laughed at for it. If you
take a foreign author's play, pay him something and acknowledge
it, even though, owing to some omission on his part, or by the
fault of the law, you are not legally compelled to do so. If you
" adapt" a man's book, let it be a straightforward, above-board
transaction. I can only see one difference myself between the
man who steals a man's purse or watch and the man who steals
a play, and that is that the latter is a coward as well as a thief,
because he knows he cannot be punished.

Do not dabble in indecencies. That sort of thing pays less
and less every year. A certain number of people, of course,
roar over them, but you do not hear the silent disgust of the
better half of the audience.

Do not write too much. I say this not in the cause of the
public, but for your own sake. A writer is not an inexhaustible
stream ; he is only a mine. He contains a certain amount of
good metal, and what comes after that is rubbish. And do not
write too quickly. A brain can't be driven like a cab horse.
Many a clever dramatist works himself to death in the
first few years of his popularity, and then has to sit aside and
know himself " played out" before his time. A man, after one

or two successes, is applied to on every side for plays. Managers, who a year ago would not look at the very pieces that have since made him famous, now crowd round him and offer him any terms to write anything. If he is wise, he shuts his ears and goes quietly in his own course. If he is foolish, "he makes haste to be rich," undertakes three or four times as much work as he is capable of properly performing, is compelled to "scamp" it, and, in consequence, turns out failure after failure.

Do not—but I will take my own advice for once, and not write too much. I have said all that is in me worth saying, perhaps more, on this matter of " playwriting." I will stop before I come to the rubbish. Good-bye, and here's luck !

APPENDIX.

In the early pages of this work, the remark was made that it is absolutely necessary for a playwright to be personally acquainted with the stage. Many readers of this book, however, will find that "going on the stage" or them is an impossibility. For the guidance and assistance of those who are unacquainted with the world behind the footlights, and wholly ignorant of "stage directions," their meaning and bearing in playwriting, this Appendix is intended. A careful study of the plans and sketches given will enable, it is hoped, all would-be dramatic authors to make the stage directions of their plots at least intelligible to the professional mind.

The first plate gives a ground plan of the stage, and its entrances as ordinarily arranged.

Appendix.

The second plate gives a perspective view of an imaginary exterior scene.

The third plate gives a ground plan of the second.

The fourth plate gives a perspective view of an imaginary interior scene.

The fifth plate gives a ground plan of the fourth.

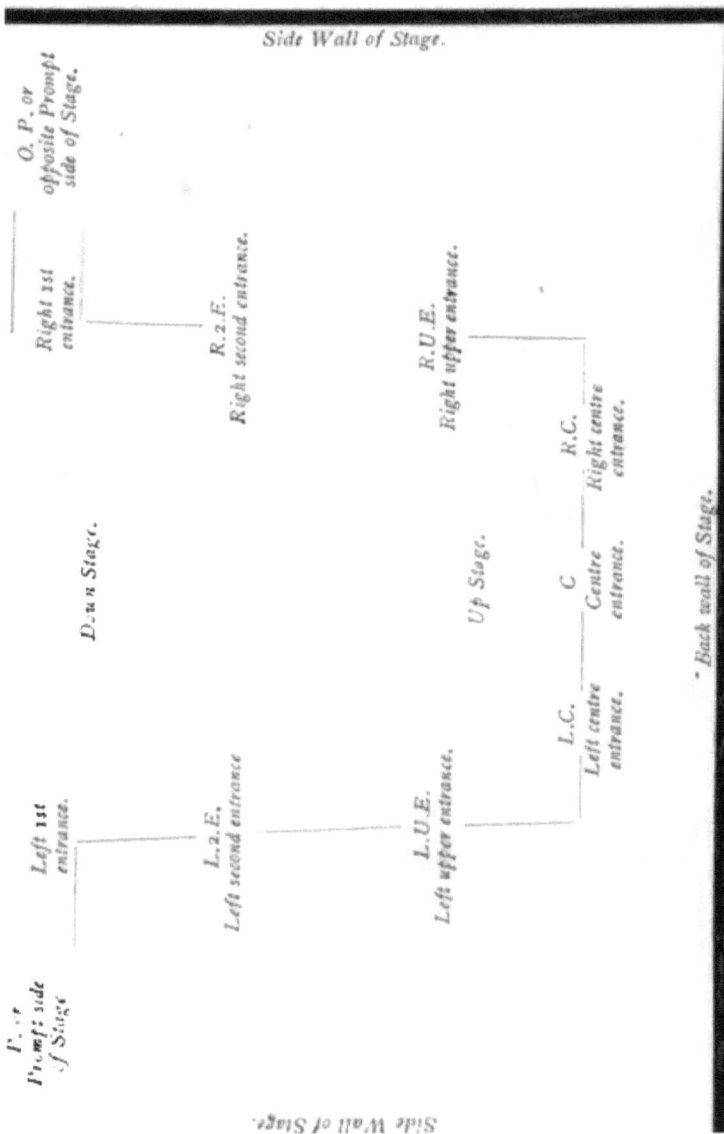

Side Wall of Stage.

O. P. or opposite Prompt side of Stage.

Right 1st entrance.

R. 2. E.
Right second entrance.

R.U.E.
Right upper entrance.

R.C.
Right centre entrance.

C
Centre entrance.

Up Stage.

Down Stage.

L.C.
Left centre entrance.

L.U.E.
Left upper entrance.

L. 2. E.
Left second entrance.

Left 1st entrance.

Prompt side of Stage.

Side Wall of Stage.

Back wall of Stage.

GENERAL PLAN OF STAGE, WITH ENTRANCES AND EXITS.

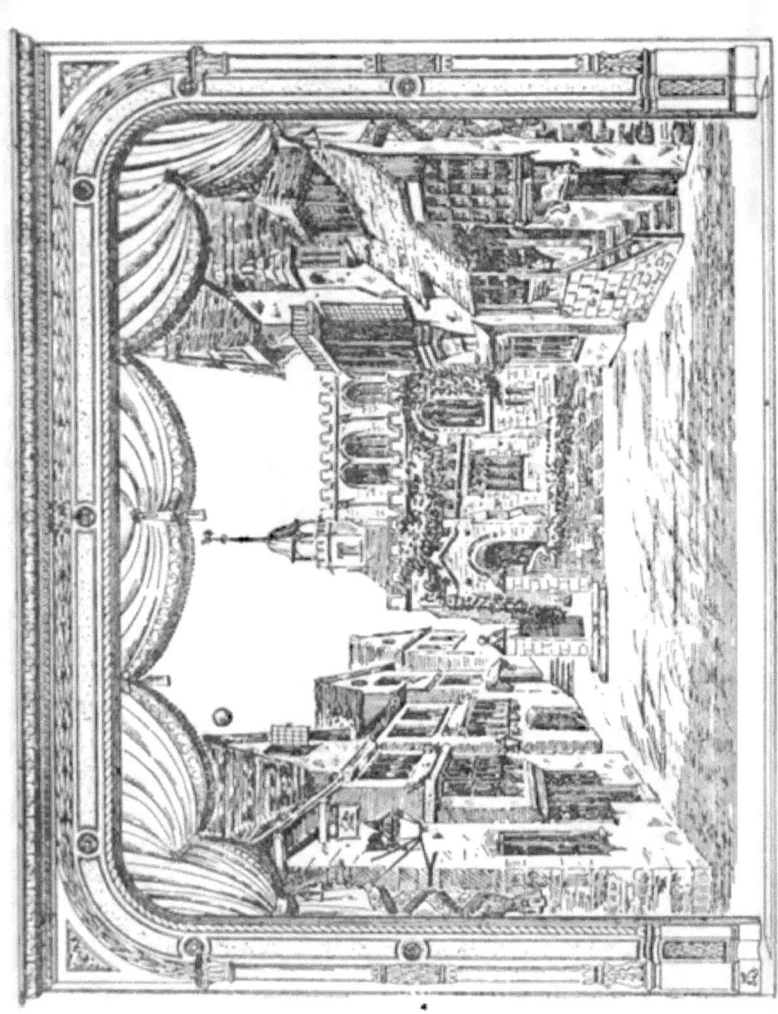

O.P.

Right 1st entrance.

R.2.E.

R.U.E.

R. C.

Porch.

Footlights.

Proscenium.

Prompt.

Left 1st entrance.

L. 2.E.

L. U. E

Back Cloth, on which is painted the Street perspective and the Horizon.

STAGE PLAN OF EXTERIOR SCENE.

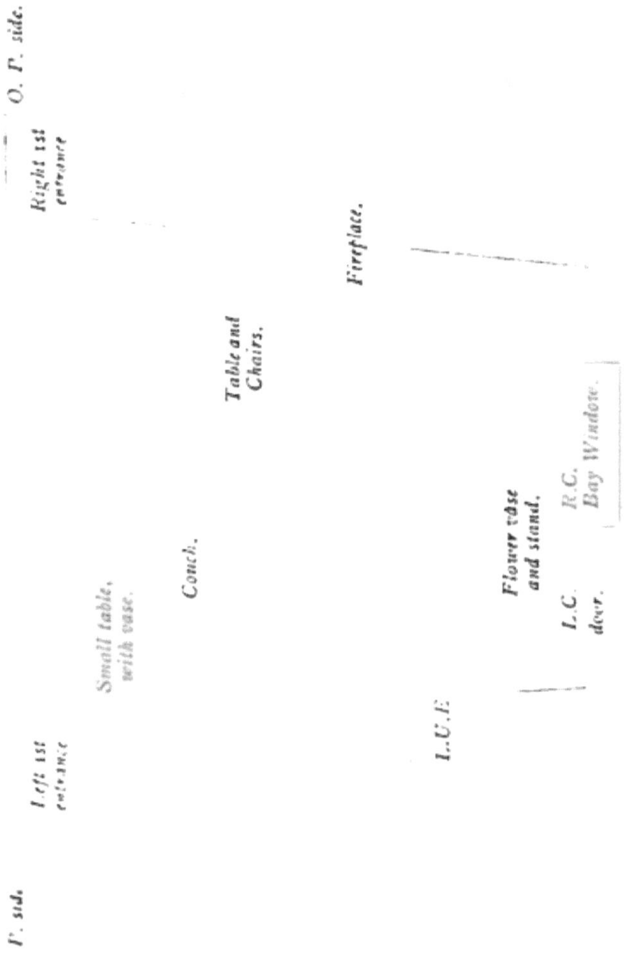

O. P. side.

Right 1st entrance

Fireplace.

Table and Chairs.

Conch.

Small table, with vase.

Flower vase and stand.

R.C. Bay Window.

L.C. door.

L.U.E.

Left 1st entrance

P. side.

www.ingramcontent.com/pod-product-compliance
Lightning Source LLC
Chambersburg PA
CBHW032013010726

47493CB00007B/2383